THE GIRL WHO RAN WITH HORSES

DAVID R. MICHAEL

Also by David R. Michael

The Girls of Spring Hollow Series
New Fairy Moon
Living Ghost Time
Tiger Girl Run
All Hollows Eve

THE GIRL WHO RAN WITH HORSES

DAVID R. MICHAEL

Published By
Four Crows Landing

For Heather

who told me
my next book should be
"abt a grl and
she is a brl rcr and
she iz jus like ME"

Chapter 1
Welcome Home, Stevie

STEVIE BUCKBEE SPENT the third wasted day of her summer vacation staring out the window at the passing Oklahoma countryside. She twisted in her seat, trying to find a comfortable position, but no longer expecting to find one. The velour of the seat had been cracked by years of sun, and the springs worn out by Aunt Mary's oversized behind.

"Do you need to use the bathroom?" Uncle Rick asked.

"No," Stevie said. She didn't look at Uncle Rick. She continued to stare out the window of the car.

Ninety minutes into the trip, and the only words Uncle Rick had spoken to her had been whether she had to pee. Once just before they pulled out of Uncle Rick's and Aunt Mary's Tulsa driveway, and just now.

"See if you can hold it another fifteen to twenty minutes," Uncle Rick said. "We're almost to McAlester."

"I'm fine," Stevie said.

Even after ten months of living in the same house, she and Uncle Rick hadn't developed any better than a functional relationship. If Aunt Mary had been in the car, the woman would have kept up a running chatter, whether anyone in the car responded or not. If her cousin April had come along, Stevie would've had someone to talk to, or at least to put between herself and her Aunt and Uncle. Eleven

1

year old April was only two years younger than Stevie, but she had no memory of Stevie's mother, and no reason to feel uncomfortable around her cousin. But Aunt Mary and cousins April, Kate, and Scottie had waved good-bye earlier, staying home, packing suitcases and getting the family SUV ready for a summer road trip. So Stevie and Uncle Rick had the car to themselves.

Silence wasn't so bad, Stevie figured. It could've been worse.

The previous Sunday, Dad had said he would drive up Thursday morning to get Stevie, take her home. Today was Saturday. Thursday evening, hours after he had been scheduled to arrive, he called to say he couldn't make it, he would be there tomorrow to get her. Tomorrow came and went with Stevie still in Tulsa, waiting. Dad called again Friday night to ask if Rick and Mary would be able to drive Stevie down to Antlers?

Uncle Rick had been livid, shouting into the phone that *his* family was leaving on a trip on Saturday and they didn't have *time*— Stopping himself, his jaw clenched, Uncle Rick handed the phone to Aunt Mary, sent a hard glare at Stevie—as if it was *her* fault, somehow—and stomped out of the living room, leaving Aunt Mary to work out a compromise with Dad.

Stevie heard only Aunt Mary's side of the conversation, but she could imagine Dad's short, simple, "No. I can't." Offering no explanation, just the repeated negation of a promise. Silent on his end of the phone while Aunt Mary, his younger sister, offered possible options until one of them met his approval. Finally, it had been decided that Uncle Rick would drive Stevie as far as McAlester, where Blake, Stevie's eighteen year old brother, would meet them and take Stevie the rest of the way.

So, yeah, Uncle Rick was upset at Dad. Stevie understood. As happy as she was to be on her way home, she was upset at Dad, as well. Two days of her summer, gone, and another ticking away. She tried not to think about it.

Because she still had time. Lots of summer remained ahead of her.

She would spend day after day with her horses, especially with Jack Rabbit and Rain and, maybe, Buckaroo. Of the three, Rain was the only one with training or experience in barrel racing, other than practice runs by Dad and Blake. But Rain was also the oldest, as old as Blake. Not too old for barrel racing, but Stevie wanted to train and race Jack Rabbit. He was *her* horse. Her first horse that was really hers, not a hand-me-down like Rain. And proof that Dad didn't break *all* his promises.

The daughter of a horse rancher and a competitive barrel racer, Stevie had never raced, had never had her own horse until Dad bought Jack Rabbit for her while she spent the school year in Tulsa. After Edwin's funeral, before Dad sent her to Tulsa with Aunt Mary and Uncle Rick, Dad had promised she would race this summer, and that he would buy her a gelding to train and race with. That her first week with Jack Rabbit over spring break had started so disastrously didn't faze her.

Her hand went to the scar on her lip before she could stop it. She forced her hand back to her lap, held it there with other hand while her lip tingled.

That hadn't been Jack Rabbit's fault. Not entirely. She and Blake had both messed up. Besides, only a trace of the split remained, where the metal shod hoof hit her, split her lip, loosened her front teeth, nearly broke her nose, and gave her a mild concussion as it sent her flying backward to land in the dust of the corral. She had lived around horses all her life and should've known better than to walk behind a skittish horse. It had been more embarrassing than painful. And it had hurt a lot.

Thrown and kicked, spending hours in the emergency room getting stitched up and scanned, and then wasting most of a week on her back as both Dad and Blake alternated between hovering over her, blaming themselves, blaming her, blaming Jack Rabbit, and refusing to let her do anything lest she hurt herself again. Spring break had *not* gone as planned.

Horse and rider had to get to used to each other, she had told both Blake and Dad over and over, until they finally allowed her and Jack Rabbit some time for riding and bonding—with Blake and Dad looking on like mother hens. Too long ago, and too short a time.

Summer, though, had finally arrived, if a couple days late. Three months that she could spend in her real home, with Blake and Dad. And, more importantly, with Jack Rabbit.

She and Jack Rabbit would race at rodeos and exhibitions and any other event in Oklahoma, Texas and Arkansas that offered barrel racing. In her dreams, she and Jack Rabbit won all of the races. But in the real world, she was prepared to place as low as third or fourth in the first few races, as she and Jack Rabbit found their stride together.

For the past two months, she had scoured the Web looking barrel racing events from June through August. Her first list contained one hundred seventeen events in ten states, encompassing a region from New Mexico to Louisiana to Iowa to Wyoming. The first time she mentioned her list to Dad, over the phone, she heard him choke on his drink and spend two full minutes coughing. She took the hint and narrowed the list down to only thirteen events, just a bit more than one a week for the entire summer. She had sent Dad and Blake emails with the final list, but she had also made four printouts of the list, one each for her, Blake and Dad, plus another for posting on the fridge.

A line of horse farms passed by on her side of the car, and pulled Stevie's attention back to the present. The heat of the Oklahoma summer had settled in, making the June morning hot and sticky outside the air-conditioning of the car, but there were still a few horses standing in the corrals and pastures, heads down, munching on green grass, or heads up, looking around.

As she watched, all the horses brought their heads up and turned to the highway. Looking at the car.

At her.

Stevie sat up, feeling an unexpected surge in her chest, her heart pounding, her eyes locked to those of a bay mare with a long black mane and three white socks. Stevie blinked, but when she opened her eyes again, she knew that the horse still looked at her. Hundreds of yards away, moving past at seventy miles an hour. Stevie shook her head. She had to be imagining it.

As if it heard her, the mare blew out—impossibly, she seemed to *hear* the blow, *feel* it on her cheek—and shook its head. And Stevie could feel the eyes of the mare and the other horses looking at her. Not at the highway, not at the cars. At *her*.

"Looking at the horses?" Uncle Rick asked, distracting her.

"What?" Stevie asked, then added, "Yes." She turned back to the window.

They had passed the horses, left them behind. She could feel the distance between her and the bay mare growing, whatever connection they had shared fading. Her heart slowed. Had she imagined it?

A green highway sign flashed by, announcing "McAlester 11" in white letters that sparkled in the late morning sun.

Another fifteen minutes, and she would see Blake. Tall, gangly, tanned, with perpetual sun streaks in his hair. Good looking too, in a dorky, brother kind of way. Not as good looking as Edwin had been. None of them had been as good looking as Edwin. Not Blake, not Dad, and certainly not Stevie. Edwin had looked more like Mom than any of them...

Stevie let those thoughts drift away. Let the tightness that squeezed her heart loosen. Before the tears could come. Tears for Edwin. Not Mom.

She resisted the urge to wipe at her eyes. Uncle Rick would probably think... whatever it was the man thought. Probably ask her—again—if she could hold it until they got to the McDonald's where Blake waited for them.

Ten minutes to Blake. She would be glad to see him. She was always glad to see Blake.

And then another hour—maybe less, the way Blake drove—and she would be home, with Jack Rabbit and the rest of her horses, for the first time in two months.

They passed a few more ranches and fields with horses. Stevie didn't feel the same connection as she had with the bay mare, but as she watched, each of the horses turned to the highway and watched her on her way home.

She tried to remember if horses always did that.

"Do you see his car?" Uncle Rick asked as they pulled in the McDonald's parking lot.

"Truck," Stevie said. She scanned for Blake's old Chevy. "No," she said. "I don't see him."

"Great," Uncle Rick said, irritation obvious in his voice. He pulled into an empty spot. "I guess we'll wait here." He settled back into the driver's seat, the engine still running.

Stevie had been about to open her door. She stopped. "Here in the car?" she asked.

"I'm not hungry," he replied.

The rumble in Stevie's stomach was drowned by that of a diesel engine as a large pickup passed behind them. Stevie turned to look over her shoulder, then smiled.

"Dad's here!" she said, forgiving the man instantly because he had come himself, and—mostly—forgiving Uncle Rick for being surly.

She opened the car door and stepped out before Uncle Rick could respond. She jumped and waved at the big green Dodge truck. "Dad!" she called. "Over here!"

The truck pulled into the nearest empty spot.

Stevie stopped walking toward the truck, stopped waving, as the passenger door opened and a woman jumped down. No, not a woman. A girl, only a few years older than Stevie.

The bubble of joy at seeing Dad burst and Stevie let her arm fall. She had been so certain that it was Dad's truck—

"Hi, Stevie," the girl said, smiling and giving Stevie a wave.

Stevie just stared at the girl. She didn't wave back, though the girl did look familiar.

The girl waited at the end of the long bed of the pickup. The man who had been driving the truck came around and put his arm around the girl. They walked toward Stevie.

"Blake?" Stevie said.

Blake grinned his famous grin. He had the same boyish look to him. Undoubtedly the same brother she had always known. But with his arm around the girl, he looked... older. Almost like she remembered Dad looking. Before.

She would've run up and hugged him. But not in front of the girl.

"Where's Dad?" Stevie asked, not moving closer, making Blake come to her.

Blake's grinned faltered, became a touch sad. "I thought he told you I was picking you up."

Beside Stevie, the trunk of Uncle Rick's car popped open.

"He did," Stevie said. "But I saw the truck and thought..." She stopped. "He let you drive his *truck*?"

"Hey, Rick," Blake said to Uncle Rick as the older man got out of the car. Blake disentangled himself from the girl and stepped over to shake Uncle Rick's hand.

Uncle Rick took Blake's hand, but gave it only a quick shake. "I'm glad you're on time," he said.

Stevie pulled her suitcase and duffel bag from the trunk without looking at the bags, her eyes on Blake and Uncle Rick. And flicking over to the girl, then back to Blake.

Blake had a *girlfriend*? When had that happened? And why hadn't he *told* her?

"Let me get those," Blake said, interrupting Stevie's thoughts.

Steve let him take the suitcase, but held onto the duffel bag. There was nothing important in the suitcase. Just clothes.

"You don't remember me, do you?" the girl asked. She gave Stevie an amused smile.

"I—" Stevie started. The girl looked so familiar, especially that infuriating smile. But nothing like any of the girls Blake had ever made eyes at, and occasionally made out with. This girl was mousy, and almost pale even with a tan, with light brown hair and green eyes. Pretty, yes, but not in Blake's league.

"See you," Blake said to Uncle Rick. He stepped between Stevie and the girl, his left hand holding the girl's right, nudging Stevie into motion by smacking her in the bottom with the flat of the suitcase.

"Hey!" Stevie protested, but started walking.

"Thanks again, Rick," Blake called over his shoulder.

Uncle Rick didn't respond. Stevie heard him get into his car. A few seconds later, the car pulled out of its spot and eased past them. Stevie waved with her free hand, but Uncle Rick still didn't respond.

Blake heaved Stevie's suitcase into the bed of the pickup, lifting it easily over the tailgate and setting it down. He gestured to the duffel bag. "You want me to put that back here too?"

Stevie pulled the duffel bag closer and gave Blake a *look*. "Stop trying to steal my personal stuff," she said.

Blake laughed. "I didn't care before, but *now* I'm curious what you have in there." He paused and looked at the girl who still held his left hand. "Stevie, you remember Shannon, don't you?"

Shannon smiled and held out her free hand to Stevie. "Oh, right," Stevie said, awkwardly shaking Shannon's left hand with her right. "Shannon Craig," she said, the name coming to her. "You're in the band. You tried to teach me how to play the clarinet."

"And failed," Blake said.

"Shut up," Stevie said, feeling her face get warm. She started to say more, to point out that a giggly sophomore was hardly the best teacher for a mature fifth grader, and, further, that the whole experience was two years ago, but her stomach rumbled again. Her face got even warmer as the others laughed.

"If you're hungry," Blake said, "we can hit the drive through. We need to get back, though."

Stevie rode in the back seat of the extended cab, feeling even more like a kid than she usually did when back there. It was different when Dad was driving, and Blake took the passenger seat—heaving her over the seat into the back when she made that necessary. Riding behind Blake and his girlfriend, the mousy Shannon, the two of them holding hands and looking at each other enough to make the big truck a danger on the highway, made her feel like an outsider, looking in.

She had been looking forward to riding back with Blake, talking to him, catching up, and telling him her big plans for the big summer. With Shannon in the truck too, though, Stevie limited herself to eating her Sausage Egg McMuffin and hash brown, slurping her orange juice, and making the shortest possible replies to questions.

She tried not to, but couldn't help but wonder how long Blake and Shannon had been going out. She didn't want to ask in front of Shannon, though. And, to be honest, she didn't want to hear a sappy story of love at first sight or an amusing coincidence. And the last thing she wanted to hear was—

"It was at the hospital, while you were getting your CAT scan," Blake said, catching Stevie's eye in the rearview mirror. "Shannon was helping out as a candy striper..."

Stevie resisted the urge to put her hands over her ears and start yelling to drown him out. The thought of Blake making out with girls had become a lot less disgusting to Stevie over the past year as Stevie found herself making eyes at—and wanting to make out with—a few of the guys at school back in Tulsa. But, still. Too much information was too much information.

They rolled into Antlers none too soon, though Blake took an unexpected turn off Main Street, before downtown, and well before their own turn, back to the ranch.

"Where we going?" Stevie asked.

"Dropping off Shannon," Blake said.

Stevie smiled. The first good news all day. She looked away as the two kissed each other good-bye, then crawled over the seat to the passenger side when Shannon abandoned it.

"You didn't respond to my email," Stevie said as they pulled out of the driveway and left the Craig's house behind.

"What?" Blake asked. "Which email?"

"The list," Stevie said.

Blake looked at her, showing no comprehension.

"The *list*," Stevie repeated. "*My* list. Of barrel racing competitions," she added when Blake still didn't get it. As if she had sent him more than one list. Well, she had. But she had clearly stated that the last list was the important one.

"Oh, right."

The tone of Blake's voice set off alarms in Stevie's head. "What?"

"We can talk about that later," Blake said. His expression shifted, became a smirk. "By the way, you had a visitor at the ranch yesterday."

"Don't try to change the subject," Stevie said. But then the smirk got her. As he knew it would. "Who?" she asked. She tried to think who it might be, feeling a touch of guilt. She hadn't kept in touch with her Antlers friends as well as she should have. Just a few emails here and there. Spending spring break first in the hospital and then bedridden most of the week hadn't helped.

"I asked him if he wanted to leave you a note or anything. But he said, no, he'd see you around." Blake stopped talking.

Stevie looked up. "Him? Him who?" None of the names she had been thinking had been a *him*.

Blake was suddenly concentrating his full attention on the road in front of them. As if it weren't broad daylight and as if something unexpected might jump out at him in this sleepy little town.

Stevie reached across and slugged Blake in the shoulder. "Who?" she demanded.

"Oww," Blake said, wincing from the blow more than was probably necessary, especially considering the size of the grin on his smug little face. "How should I know? I can't keep your boyfriends straight— Oww!" he said again as Stevie hit him again.

Stevie cocked her fist for another blow. "Who was it?"

Blake laughed. Then he took the turn back onto Main Street faster and sharper than he had to, the force of the turn pushing Stevie back into her seat.

"Wrong answer," she said. She leaned toward him and hit him again.

Blake only laughed louder. "OK OK," he said, as Stevie drew back her fist once more. Still grinning, though. Stevie thought about hitting him again, just on principle. But Blake finally gave in. "It was Travis Delozier."

Stevie dropped her raised fist. "Who?"

Blake gave her a sideways look. "You were only gone a year—not even a full year. And you've forgotten everybody already? First Shannon, now Travis." He smirked again. "You do know who I am, right? Your brother, Blake? And not just some handsome stranger? And you're not going to run away scared from Dad, are you?"

"Shut up," Stevie said. "Whoever said you were handsome?" She thought about hitting Blake in the shoulder again, but realized he was probably keeping score. No way he was letting her punch him that many times without some kind of retaliation. "Travis? How did he even know I was coming home?"

"Oh," Blake said, his face taking on that innocent look of his. "Well, he had come by last week too. He asked then."

"Travis?" Stevie asked again. "Why would Travis... ?" Thoughts of Edwin flooded her mind. Edwin and Travis together at the ranch, running and riding, at school, laughing, before the accident. "He was *Edwin's* friend. And I was..." She stopped.

"Steevie Creevie," Blake supplied. "The Pest."

"Shut up," Stevie said, her mouth on autopilot. Edwin had given her that name, Steevie Creevie, when she was three. And added "the pest" when he was eight and she was six.

Blake turned the truck onto the county road that led to the ranch. The familiar turn, the sense that home and Dad—and her horses!—were so close, brought Stevie back to more important matters.

"Whatever," she said. The mystery of Travis Delozier could wait. "I know I've lost two days this week, but maybe we can make up one of them tomorrow. The first race on the list is next Thursday, in Hugo. I was hoping to have a full week back in the saddle by then, and getting Jack Rabbit ready. I'm not sure how well we'll do, that soon after..." She trailed off as she noticed Blake shaking his head. "What?" she asked.

Blake shook his head a few more seconds before saying, "It won't work, Stevie." He held up his right hand, palm almost in her face to forestall her response. "Wait. You've only just got home. Enjoy it for a few days before—"

"But I want to *ride*," she said. "And race."

"There will be plenty of races this summer—"

"One hundred and seventeen," Stevie said.

"—and I'll try to help you as much as I can," Blake went on. He stopped, and threw her a puzzled look. "One hundred seventeen? That's more than one a day."

Stevie looked away, shrugged. "I didn't plan to go to *all* of them—"

"Good," Blake said. "I'll try to help you as much as I can," he said again.

They reached the front gate of the ranch. Stevie noticed that the metal gate hadn't been given a new coat of white paint this year. The metal letters announcing "The Buckbee Horse Ranch" showed signs of wear, and a few spots of rust. Had the gate been that worn looking over spring break? She didn't remember.

"But tomorrow," Blake went on. He paused for a second, then continued, "I've already got plans."

"Plans? What kind of plans?"

Blake didn't answer, just kept talking. "And there's no way we could be ready to go to a race next week. You'll need to give me a few weeks—"

"A few weeks? That's almost a *month*. I'd miss three races by then—"

"—to get everything—" He looked at her. "You were wanting to go to a race every *week*?"

"Not *every* week," Stevie said. She bit her lip. "OK, yes, every week. And one week had two races. But it's the last week of the summer," she added, quickly, so that Blake wouldn't think she was being unreasonable.

Blake snorted. "You're going to have to talk to Dad about this," he said, pulling up in front of the two story house, their home. He put the truck in park, set the emergency brake, and opened the door. He closed the door behind him, walked to the front door of the house.

Stevie sat there in the cab of the truck, watching him walk away. That hadn't gone at all the way she planned. Blake was supposed to be as enthusiastic as she was, excited even. She needed him to help her. If she had to count on Dad, she'd never—

No, that was unkind. Dad would help her. Some. But never as much as he promised. And not enough. She needed Blake.

The front door of the house opened and Dad stepped out. He wore his typical blue jeans and t-shirt and muddy boots, hair disheveled, eyes blinking at the bright sunlight. He looked around, saw Stevie still in the truck. She saw his mouth move, but couldn't hear him. He smiled, though, so she smiled back and waved, then opened the door to get out.

"What were you waiting for, Stevie?" Dad asked as he came around the truck. "Looking for a red carpet, maybe? You weren't gone *that* long."

Stevie pulled her duffel bag out of the back seat, then turned to face Dad. She should be mad at him for not picking her up two days in a row—and she was, some—but she was glad to see him. She hugged him, putting her face against his chest. He smelled of sweat and horses and manure and hay. With just a hint of scotch.

He returned the hug, a tight squeeze, then released her.

"Blake didn't get your suitcase?" he asked. "Damn it, Blake," he said, raising his voice, looking to the front of the house. "You didn't get Stevie's suitcase." He reached into the bed of the pickup and pulled the suitcase over the side.

"Did *you* get my email?" Stevie asked. "The one with the list of races this summer?"

"Yeah," Dad said. "Looked like a long list."

"It's only thirteen races," Stevie protested. "But Blake said he wouldn't be able to help me train for almost a whole month. And there's a race next week, and the week after—"

"Blake's been busy," Dad said, using his voice and the heavy sounds of his boots on the porch steps to override Stevie. "Barely has time for anything now."

Stevie stopped just outside the front door. "Then who's going to help me train?" she asked. "Who's going to take me to the races?"

Dad shrugged. "We'll figure something out," he said. He opened the glass storm door, and walked into the air-conditioned darkness of the house. The storm door closed behind him, leaving Stevie on the porch, looking at herself in the reflection of the glass, alone, still waiting for a reply.

Chapter 2
Stevie Runs

"DID YOU FORGET your key?" Blake asked, pushing open the glass door and holding it for her. He gave her a smile, a peace offering.

Stevie looked at him. She rejected the peace offering and didn't smile back. "I have my key," she said. "I'm just not sure this is the home it goes to. Not *my* home, anyway."

"Don't get pissy," Blake said, his smile fading.

"Why would I be pissy?" Stevie asked. "Just because no one cares that my plans for the summer are being ruined?"

"You're not the only one with plans," he said. The smile was gone now. He started to say more, but didn't. "Are you coming in, or not?"

"Damn it, Blake," Dad said, coming down the stairs behind Blake. "Don't stand there with door open." He didn't stop at the bottom of the stairs, but walked into the front room that had been the office of the ranch as long as Stevie could remember.

Blake shrugged and came out the door. He still held the door open for Stevie. "You going in?" he asked.

"Where are you going?" Stevie asked.

"To the tractor barn."

Now Stevie smiled. Blake hated working on the old tractor. "Have fun."

"Oh, yeah." Blake let go of the door as Stevie stepped through, the heavy glass pane hitting her shoulder, the hydraulics of the door pushing her the rest of the way into the house.

She stood in the foyer, by herself, clutching her duffel bag. She heard Dad in the office on her left, a clink of glass, a sound of liquid pouring, another clink as the stopper went back into the bottle, then the rustle of papers being adjusted. Nothing moved in the bright, empty family room to her right, the furniture dusty and unused.

She heard Dad take a drink and put the glass back down on his desk. She listened to him mutter under his breath as he rustled more papers, looking for something.

She smelled the scents of the house, the remnants of breakfast, the ever present musk of horses, a hint of Blake's aftershave.

She was home now. Somehow, the thought of *home* wasn't as exciting as it had been. And the big house seemed emptier than she ever remembered it feeling, even in the days right after Edwin died. Friends and family had been in and out, then the funeral, then Stevie was heading to Tulsa with Uncle Rick and Aunt Mary. There hadn't been time for the house to feel empty. Now, though...

Dad appeared in the archway to the office. He had a small glass with his drink in his left hand. In his right he held an envelope by the corner.

"You got a card," he said, holding the envelope out to her. "Came back in January, on your birthday. Forgot to give it to you when you were down last."

Stevie stared at the envelope. She didn't want to take it.

"Take it," Dad said. "It's from your mother."

Stevie knew who it was from. Still, she reached for the envelope, took it, the paper feeling cool against her fingers. She turned it over to look at the postmark. *Wyoming.* Same as it had been the last few years. Before that had been Montana. Once it had been California. As always, there was no return address. Just her name, "Miss Stevie Buckbee," and the address of the ranch, written in purple ink, Mom's handwriting as perfect as it ever was.

She turned and started up the stairs.

"Aren't you going to open it?" Dad asked.

Stevie nodded. She didn't want to. But she knew she would. She always did. She continued up the stairs. Behind her, she heard Dad go back into the office, take a drink and, after a few seconds, pull the chair out from his desk and sit down.

Her room looked exactly as she had left it two months ago. Her bed remained mussed from the last night she had slept in it over spring break. The stack of books beside the bed hadn't been disturbed, nor any of the stuffed animals that had been left behind to fend for themselves. Like the family room below, a thin layer of dust had settled over everything. Only her suitcase, which Dad had propped up beside the bed, was dust free.

The stuffed animals, the books, the bed, the room, everything, looked smaller. As if her room had shrunk while she was away.

While at Aunt Mary's and Uncle Rick's, she had shared a room with April. Stevie had been looking forward to having her own room again, a room to herself. Just like she had been looking forward to being home.

And here she was. Home, in her own room. And she felt just as alone as she had all year. She didn't miss April or Kate or Scottie—certainly not Scottie. And not Aunt Mary or Uncle Rick. Dad and Blake were here. But still she felt... alone.

She looked at the unopened envelope in her hand, then at the stack of birthday cards on the shelf above her bed. Seven birthday cards—eight now—all the contact she had had with Mom in as many years. Mom, letting Stevie know that she hadn't forgotten her. Reminding Stevie every year, on her birthday, of what she had lost.

Her thirteenth birthday had been spent in Tulsa. Aunt Mary had baked a yellow cake mix, topped it with chocolate icing from a can, and put candles on it, like she did for all her kids. Stevie had blown out the candles, forced down her piece of cake with a smile, and cried herself to sleep that night, quietly, so that April wouldn't hear. Even without a birthday card, Stevie remembered. She didn't want to remember her birthday. Or Mom.

She threw her duffel bag onto the bed, dropped the unopened birthday card on top of it, and left the room, headed down the stairs. At least she still had her horses.

"Stevie?" Dad called from the office just as she came off the stairs and stepped to the front door.

She stopped, hand on the latch. "Yeah?"

"The horses are in the south pasture today," Dad said. "Blake's supposed to be mowing the north pastures."

"OK." Stevie pushed through the door and into the early summer heat.

She went to the big stable first and raided a handful of the carrots kept there in a bin. She had to reach in and run her fingers across the bottom of the bin, and only came up with four rather unimpressive carrots. She had hoped for more, but this would do for now.

The south pasture was the largest part of the ranch. It had been subdivided into two large, square-ish fields, instead of the many long grazing strips of the north pastures. Stevie hadn't noticed the horses in the pasture on the way in, so they must be in the southeast corner where the dust from Blake's mowing wouldn't be as much of an irritation. For her as well as the horses.

She walked down the narrow, fenced path that divided the southeast and southwest pastures until she saw the first cluster of horses, about a ten of them, mares and geldings. As one, the horses stopped grazing and looked at her.

Stevie's spoken greeting fizzled on her lips, and she felt self-conscious. "Uh... hey," she managed to say, resisting the urge to look behind her, to see what the horses had to be looking at.

A few of the horses nickered in response, and another few bobbed their heads.

Stevie stood there. For the first time in her life she was unsure how to behave around horses. First being thrown and kicked by Jack Rabbit on spring break. Now, greeted in this very uncustomary way by a small herd.

After a long minute, some of the horses bobbed their heads again, and all of them went back to what they had been doing before Stevie walked up.

Stevie realized her mouth hung open, and closed it. Then she realized that Jack Rabbit wasn't among the group of horses. None of the ranch's own horses stood with the group.

She started to ask, "Where's Jack Rabbit?" Not because she expected an answer, just being friendly with the horses. But she stopped after "Where's..."

Because a blue roan gelding, Satchmo, who had been stabled at the ranch for the last five years, looked up again, and gestured with a swing of his neck and nose to his left, Stevie's right. An image of Jack Rabbit, prancing around and looking proud and foolish, flashed into her mind.

Closing her open mouth once more, Stevie turned to look in the indicated direction—indicated not just by the pointing nose of Satchmo, but a pull in her head that felt for all the world like Blake taking her head in his hands, as he used to do, and forcing her to look where he wanted her to look. She almost said, "Stop it!" to the absent Blake.

The world seemed to tilt in front of her, and she stumbled.

She found herself reliving the long, slow, painful moment over spring break when Jack Rabbit threw her off. Jack Rabbit had bucked Stevie out of the saddle, then kicked her. All Stevie could remember was getting up after being thrown, moving to help Blake get Jack Rabbit under control, seeing Jack Rabbit hunch, then feeling the shock, breathing the dust as she lay on the packed earth of the corral, staring up at the sky, one eye swelling shut while she tasted blood, wondering if she had lost any teeth, and wondering which hoof had hit her.

Stevie licked her lips, almost surprised to find no swelling gash, no taste of blood. The scar above her left eye tingled. The world lurched again, and she caught herself on the nearest wooden fence post and held onto it while the world tried to buck her off.

As she clung to the fence post, fighting the sudden urge to throw up, she wondered if she should go back to the house. Maybe she was sick.

It wasn't fair. She had only just got home. She *couldn't* be sick. There was too much to do this summer for her to be sick. And if she told Dad, he would probably restrict her from the horses. At the least, it would be a reason for him and Blake to withdraw even more support for her racing plans.

She took in a deep breath, let it out slow. The world still spun, but now at less than breakneck speed.

Maybe she was scared of Jack Rabbit now? She rejected the thought at once. The fault had been hers, and maybe Blake's. Both of them should've known better.

And Dad had made a rare trip to Tulsa, to bring her home for the weekend, a week after spring break, two weeks after the accident, to help her get back in the saddle. Back in Jack Rabbit's saddle, to be specific. Jack Rabbit had been nervous, just like her, but they both got over it. Dad and Blake had been there too, probably more nervous than girl and horse combined. They got over it too. Stevie had gone back to school to finish the spring semester. She had been confident again, and making big plans for the summer.

Stevie stood up straight, but still clung to the fence post. She blinked a couple times, then released the post, keeping her hand close to it, ready to grab it again.

Satisfied that the world was behaving once more, Stevie looked up and saw another group of horses, fifty yards or so away. Right where Satchmo had said—

The world threatened to heave into motion again. Stevie squeezed her eyes shut and shook her head to clear it, her hands still ready to latch onto the fence post again, if that proved necessary.

She opened her eyes. The group of horses had not moved, but they were looking at her now. She could see Jack Rabbit's head. And she saw Rain and Buckaroo and Hobo and more, a group of about fifteen.

Stevie looked at Satchmo and the others of the nearer group, and counted eleven. Only twenty-five to thirty horses? Last summer, there had been fifty-six horses stabled at the Buckbee Horse Ranch. She scanned the pasture, what she could see of it, but didn't see any other horses. Where were the rest?

Still not sure if she could trust the world to remain stable, Stevie took a first step along the fence toward the second group of horses. The world made no sudden moves, and after a couple more cautious steps, Stevie felt like herself again.

Only Rain watched Stevie's progress down the fence. The other horses, including Jack Rabbit, had gone back to grazing and flicking. A small stab of sadness poked her heart that only Rain watched her. She loved Rain, of course. But Jack Rabbit was supposed to be hers, Stevie's. And Jack Rabbit hardly seemed aware of her.

Stevie came to the point where she was directly across from the horses. Here the wooden slats gave way to a wide gate. Stevie climbed to the top slat, ignoring the groans of protest in the old wood, and balanced there, propping herself with her heels on the next lower slat.

She frowned at her sneakers. City habit. In her excitement—in the rush to get out of her room—she had forgotten to put on her boots. She needed new boots anyway, her boots from last summer would be too small. Maybe Blake could take her into town tomorrow. Or Monday. She couldn't remember if the shoe store was open on Sunday. That was one advantage a bigger place like Tulsa had over dinky little Antlers: shoe stores were open seven days a week.

Putting sneakers, boots, and especially Tulsa out of her mind, Stevie looked at the horses. Rain had gone back to grazing, but the old mare, an Appaloosa with a blanket of spots across her back and hips, looked up again and caught Stevie's eye.

Stevie smiled for Rain. "Hey, girl," she said.

Rain had been at the ranch for a long time. Longer than all of the other horses, certainly longer than Stevie. Stevie had learned to ride on Rain, and run her first barrel races with the mare. At eighteen, Rain was five years older than Stevie. Old enough, in horse years, to be Stevie's mother. Rain had been Mom's horse, and left behind with the rest of them the day Mom didn't come home.

Rain snorted then, and shifted, brushing against the other horses, making her way out of the group toward Stevie.

Stevie pushed these new thoughts about Mom aside— back behind the wall she had built for them—and sat up straighter, smiled wider. But the horse only came halfway.

Rain stopped about fifteen feet away.

Sadness welled up in Stevie. "Rain," she said. "Not you too..." Blake, and Dad, and Jack Rabbit, and now Rain. Everyone keeping their distance. Her big summer was off to a lousy start.

Rain snorted and stamped her right hoof hard enough to send up a small dust cloud.

Unbidden memories of Mom flashed in Stevie's mind. *Don't just sit there crying, Stevie. Come here. Tell me what's wrong.* Mom's voice, speaking to little Stevie, maybe three years old. Stevie blinked, saw Rain again.

The mare nodded at her then stamped her hoof again, though softer this time.

Images in her mind again, but now of Stevie jumping down from the fence, offering Rain a carrot, running full tilt with her hair streaming behind her as Rain trotted alongside her.

Stevie felt the bulge of the carrots in her jeans and gave Rain a small laugh. "Sorry, girl," she said. "I forgot I had those." She took out a carrot and held it out.

Rain snorted, shook her head, but then took a step toward Stevie. Another. Rain stopped again and looked at Stevie.

Stevie sighed. "What's the matter, girl?" she asked. She mustered another smile. "Do I smell funny?"

Horses don't shrug, but the combination of short steps and the head bob came across as a shrug and a "Maybe," poking fun at her.

Stevie laughed then. She pushed off the top of the fence and jumped down. The old wood of the fence protested such rough treatment and her shoes raised little dust clouds as she landed. Rain waited for her as she walked up.

Stevie raised her hand to stroke Rain's neck, offering the carrot with the other hand. But the horse just snorted. Stevie hesitated, started to draw back.

Rain stepped forward then, head weaving around Stevie's hand to rest on her shoulder, almost knocking her over.

Surprised but happy, Stevie hugged Rain around the neck, squeezing as tight as she could, trying not to cry.

She heard other hooves approaching, then her other ear got nuzzled. Jack Rabbit, still apologizing, it seemed. Stevie shifted her hug to him. "It's OK, boy, I know you didn't mean it."

I'm glad you're home. A woman's voice in her head. Not Mom's. Not a voice Stevie recognized, not right away, but she didn't worry about it. At least somebody was glad she was home. Even if it was an imaginary voice in her head. A voice that made her remember being a child.

"Me too," she said.

She felt Jack Rabbit chewing on the back of her pants, and then the horse came away with one of the carrots. He backed away from her, then pranced a short dance. Stevie laughed. "I was going to give you one of those."

She pulled the rest of the carrots from her back pocket before the other horses followed Jack Rabbit's lead—

Rain and a couple of the other horses snorted, surprising her.

Not sure what she wasn't understanding, Stevie gave the first carrot to Rain while stroking her nose. "Did you miss me, girl?"

A warm feeling wrapped itself around Stevie and she knew that *of course* she had been missed. How could her horses not miss her? How could she have stayed away so long?

"It wasn't my idea," Stevie said. "I wanted to stay here."

She broke the rest of the carrots in pieces and gave them to as many of the other horses as she could, starting with Buckaroo and Hobo and Scamper and Buttermilk.

Jack Rabbit nosed his way back into the circle of horses around her, looking for seconds. She tapped him on the nose and said, "Greedy." She laughed at the expression on his face, and gave him an extra piece anyway.

When she had no carrots left, the horses still shifted around her. Stevie picked up on the skittish vibe, and followed the heads of the horses and looked at the fence.

A boy stood there, leaning against fence where she had sitting. She recognized his face, though it had changed some in the past year. His hair was longer, shaggier if that was possible. His face was longer too, less round, becoming the face of a man. And the cuts and abrasions on his face and arms from the accident had long healed.

But she didn't just see Travis Delozier.

Hey, Steevie Creevie!

Beside Travis, sitting on the fence, Edwin smiled and looked as if he had just called out her childhood name— the name he had given her. Edwin hadn't aged like Travis. Edwin was still the fourteen year old version of himself from last summer. With the angelic face she could still see in her memories and in pictures. From before the accident, before the coroner had had to reconstruct his face from some of those pictures, before he looked like a pale, sleeping, faded mannequin dressed in Edwin's clothes.

The vision of Edwin faded, leaving Travis alone by the fence, and Stevie alone in the midst of her horses.

But the jolt of sadness, and a renewed shock of loss and fear coursed through Stevie. And from and to and through the horses, as well, who stamped and snorted and pranced.

She didn't remember starting to run. Couldn't remember if the horses ran because of her, or if she ran because of them. But there was no question of whether or not to run. When you're a part of the herd, you don't stop to ask if you should or shouldn't run, or pause to find out what it is you're running from. When the herd runs, you run.

And Stevie ran.

She didn't know how, but she ran. She kept up with the horses. Every stride her foot coming down hard, raising a small cloud of dust, pushing back against the earth, thrusting her forward. Between each stride a brief sensation of flying through the air, unstoppable. Breathing in time with her stride, pulling in lungs full of air before blowing them back out again.

Girl and horses streamed across the pasture, a rolling thunder of hooves covering the sounds of her feet and breathing. The other horses grazing there looked up and whinnied and neighed as they approached. The gelding Satchmo reared as they passed, and then all of the horses of the Buckbee ranch ran together.

With Stevie.

The feelings of loss and fear goaded her, urged her to run faster, to get away from the danger, to keep up, prodded her to even greater effort. Her heart hammered in her chest as she breathed deeper than she had ever breathed in her life.

This isn't happening. The thought hit her mind and she nearly stumbled. Her misstep rippled through the herd and she found herself further back.

But still running with the horses.

The impossibility of her matching pace with a galloping horse—even a cantering horse—refused to leave her, defying the blur of the ground beneath her, the shocks of her feet against that ground, the sight of the glistening coats stretching and flexing around her.

She felt Rain beside her, knew, somehow, that the mare had kept pace with her, even as Stevie slipped back, offering support.

How many times had she dreamed of running with horses? Countless times. A little girl's fantasy.

Maybe, she thought, she was still in the car with Uncle Rick, sleeping and dreaming through the boring ride home. And she would wake up soon, her heart racing, but only from excitement. She would be so disappointed.

Stevie decided she didn't care.

The sadness and the fear drained out of her, pumped out of her, blew out of her, as she ran, left behind in the dust of the pasture. And then she ran for the joy of running.

She let out a slow, lingering whoop and holler of pure joy. She wondered if she made that sound in her sleep, startling poor Uncle Rick. She laughed and decided that she didn't care about that either.

She pumped her arms as she ran on her two legs among the horses that ran on their four. Stevie held her head high and felt her hair streaming behind her like the manes of the horses around her. Like the vision she had seen when greeting Rain.

The horses turned at the northwest corner of the pasture, curving eastward. She pulled up through the ranks of the herd again, to the front, where Jack Rabbit and Buckaroo and Satchmo vied to be the leader. Rain stayed with her until Stevie moved between Jack Rabbit and Buckaroo.

Jack Rabbit rolled his eyes at her and Stevie laughed again at his surprise to see her there, running beside him.

Stevie felt the power of Jack Rabbit's muscles as they ran, breathed when he breathed, smelled the intense smells of the pasture grasses and flowers and the familiar musks of the other horses and the diesel smoke of the old tractor and the first hints of cut grass. And she heard, as she had never heard before, the sound of hooves on grass and packed trails and the heartbeats of the herd and the sound of the tractor motor and the brush hog behind it, even the sound of the front door opening and Dad's footsteps on the porch.

She came back to herself just in time to see the northeast corner of the pasture, and subtly adjust her body and gait to make the turn. But Jack Rabbit still looked at her. As she slowed to take the turn, he sped up, to pull in front of her.

Stevie realized that he hadn't seen the turn. She started to say his name. "Jaaack—"

Time stretched as Jack Rabbit saw the corner and realized that he was going too fast.

"Raaaaab—"

The horse leaned over in slow motion as his right hoof came down, stretched out in front of him, took all of his weight in preparation for a hairpin turn.

"—bbbbiiiiiit!" She felt his right front fetlock begin to buckle under the strain. "No!" The sound in her head elongated and the "o" drew out impossibly long.

She reached out with her hand in a too slow and useless gesture, wanting to brace the fetlock, her happiness dying at full speed inside her as she faced the drawn out threat of an injury to her horse. Her dream had become a nightmare.

Her dream. Only a dream, she reminded herself. But *her* dream.

The slow motion around her crawled to a stop. She stood in a runners pose in a tableau of running horses, dust suspended in the air, Jack Rabbit just touching down in front of her.

She must be about to wake up. But before that could happen—

She imagined that she gave her strength to Jack Rabbit, her leg inside his and taking the punishing burden of turning his weight along the line of the fence. And she let the dream run full speed again.

Her right ankle exploded with pain and she screamed. Her legs buckled under her and she flew forward, watching the ground come up to meet her. Before she reached the ground, though, she fell into darkness.

A hand propped Stevie's head, fingers warm against her neck, and the fingers of another hand brushed her hair out of her eyes. She smelled dust and horses, felt the sunshine and the breath of a boy on her face.

"Stevie!" A boy's voice. "Are you OK?"

Stevie wasn't sure how to respond. This wasn't how she expected to wake up. She tried to say, "Uncle Rick," but heard herself say, "Mmm?" Her eyes were still closed.

"Oh, god," the boy's voice said, different now. Maybe relieved that she had made a noise. Or maybe even more scared than before. Stevie couldn't tell. "Are you hurt bad? Should I go get your dad?"

"Hurt?" Stevie asked. "Dad?" Images of getting home flashed in her mind. Dad talking at her and smiling at her through the truck windshield. Dad carrying her suitcase into the house. Dad with a drink and the birthday card from Mom. But how could she be home already? She had been dreaming of her horses on the ride home with Uncle Rick. "No," she said. "Don't... Dad... OK..." That hadn't come out at all how she wanted.

Stevie opened her eyes. "Augh," she said, and closed them again. Because the sunlight stabbed into her eyes and her head ached and her shoulder hurt and maybe an elbow and a knee, as well, and she could feel her right ankle throbbing painfully with every beat of her heart. And her heart chose that moment to start beating even faster because Travis Delozier had her head in his hands and was leaning over her.

This wasn't at all how she expected to wake up.

She was suddenly very much aware of Travis's warm hand against her neck, and his fingertips on her forehead, and his presence beside her on the ground of the pasture.

Stevie rolled to her side, away from Travis, ignoring

the protests of her arms and legs. She kept her eyes closed until she had pushed herself into a sitting position. Then she opened them slowly.

Travis Delozier was on his knees a few feet away from her, propping himself on his left arm, the knuckles of his left hand in the dirt where her head had been. He looked at her. "Are you sure you're OK?"

She was in the pasture. That much was obvious. The south pasture, in the northeast corner. Not only could she see it, she could smell it, and feel it where she had fallen against it. And taste it. Fortunately, just dirt and grass. Still, she spit out the grit.

She wiped her mouth with the back of her hand. "What...?"

A warm nose nuzzled her shoulder, her right shoulder, the one that didn't hurt. Stevie knew it was Rain without having to look. She hooked her right arm around to stroke the side of Rain's nose. "I'm OK, girl," she said. Looking at Travis again. "What...," she said again. She changed her question from *What are you doing here?* To, "What happened?"

Another warm nose bumped into her left shoulder, hard enough to make her wince. Jack Rabbit. "Hey, boy. You OK?" She had been dreaming, hadn't she? She couldn't have been running with the horses, not that fast. Her right ankle, though, continued to remind her that *something* had happened. And the rest of her aches and pains and the scuffs on her clothes all attested to the same thing—

"You were running," Travis said. "Then you... fell."

"Just me? Did any of the horses...?"

Travis shook his head. "They kept running. I'm surprised you didn't get kicked."

"My horses wouldn't kick me," Stevie said, and planted a kiss on Jack Rabbit's nose. "I'm just glad you didn't get hurt, boy."

Jack Rabbit pulled his nose back.

Stevie leaned over, propping herself to stand up. Travis

moved closer, offering a hand. Stevie almost took it, but then Rain had her head under Stevie's right arm, helping her stand.

Right ankle and right knee both protested the mistreatment, and Stevie hugged Rain's neck to stay upright.

Stevie looked around, and saw that most of the horses— no, she knew it was all of them, even without counting— stood around, looking at her and Travis. Only Jack Rabbit and Rain stood near, but she could feel the worry, mixed with some morbid curiosity, like bystanders at a car wreck, from the other horses.

Buckaroo caught her eye, nickered at her, a reassuring sound, happy to see she was back on her feet. Stevie smiled.

"Are you sure you don't want me to get your dad?" Travis asked, pulling Stevie's attention from Buckaroo. Travis had stood up too. He hovered nearby, looking like he wanted to help, his hands in front of him, ready, but unsure.

"Yes," Stevie said. "I mean, no, don't call him." She had no idea what she would tell Dad. She wasn't at all sure she knew what had happened. But getting hurt the first hour back on the ranch would make Dad—and Blake too—very paranoid. "I just need to..."

She wasn't sure what she needed. Fortunately, Rain seemed to have an idea. Stevie kept her right arm around Rain's neck, using the horse as a walking crutch, as the two of them walked toward the central fence.

Travis looked unconvinced, but he didn't say anything. He walked beside her, one hand ready to help.

"I'll be alright," she said. "I just need to sit down."

Jack Rabbit pranced alongside her. Stevie smiled for the big horse, but then caught the impression that he was laughing at her, ribbing her. As if telling her that she should learn how to run, and watch where she was going.

"A horse has to know how to run," Stevie said, repeating the words that came into her mind.

Jack Rabbit nodded then, and nickered, still laughing at her.

Rain snorted. So did Buckaroo and a few of the other horses.

Jack Rabbit nickered again, another laugh, at her and the other horses, then he cantered away from them.

Stevie watched Jack Rabbit move away and smiled again. His red chestnut coat glistened under the bright sunlight, and the muscles moved with easy power. She loved watching Jack Rabbit—even when he was making fun of her. Then she wondered how she had known the horse was making fun of her, and her smile faltered.

They reached the central fence, and Stevie transferred her hold from Rain's neck to the nearest fence post. She tested her right leg again, wincing even before she needed to. Her ankle didn't seem to be swelling, but it still hurt. A lot. She forced her knee to flex. It moved, if slowly, and seemed to be improving already.

She looked down at her herself and made a face. "I'm a mess," she said. And she was. Dirt and grass everywhere.

"Hang on to the post," Travis said.

That was all the warning she got. In the next instant, Stevie was clinging to the post to avoid being knocked over as Travis brushed off her back and legs, his hands slapping against her brusquely, setting off a cloud dust that made her cough.

"Stop," she managed to choke out, uncomfortable with how aware of his hands she was. "Stop it."

Travis stepped back and met her eye. His eyes were brown, she saw. She had known that for years, of course. She had seen his eyes thousands of times. But she had never noticed the particular shade of brown, or the gold flecks. She stopped looking at his eyes and just glared at him.

The corners of his lips tugged upward, as if to smile, then he looked away. The trace of smile disappeared.

"Thanks," Stevie said. "I guess." She stopped glaring at him to consider the fence. She eyed the fence post and the faded wooden slats. She wondered if maybe—

"Are you going to need help getting over the fence?"

"No," Stevie said, stopping the thought that had almost formed. She would get over this fence, or through it, one way or another, *without* Travis Delozier's help.

Behind her, Rain nickered.

Stevie looked over her shoulder at the horse. "What are you laughing at?"

Rain's expression went blank, as innocent as a newborn colt, and the horse just looked back at her.

Her ankle still protested too much to let her climb the fence post and drop on the other side. She considered walking down to the gate, but that would be long a walk away from the house—a walk she would have to then make all the back—

"Come on, I'll help," Travis said. Then he had his left arm around her waist, and was walking her along the fence to the gate.

She protested, and pulled away, so that his arm didn't wrap around her. And then grabbed his arm with both her hands when she tried to put weight on her right foot. She held onto him like that until they reached the gate.

She thought she heard Rain nicker again, but when she looked over at the horse, the mare munched idly on a clump of fescue, seeming to ignore both Stevie and Travis.

Once she was through the gate, Stevie said, "I hope Dad didn't see us." Or Blake, she didn't add.

Travis pulled the gate back into place as she stood there, leaning on a gatepost.

"So," Stevie said as Travis turned to look at her again. "Why did you... did you want to see me? Blake said..." Her voice trailed off as Travis looked at her. He smiled, but he looked sad. She couldn't help but miss Edwin when he looked like that.

Stevie looked away. Memories of Edwin suddenly seemed all around her. Like they had when she came back for Thanksgiving. Dad had sent her to Tulsa for school the day after the funeral. Coming back after nearly three months away, she kept expecting to see Edwin everywhere.

But there was no one there whenever she looked. Just her and Dad and Blake.

Stevie realized now that she had never thought of how Edwin's death had affected Travis. How had the last year been for him?

But she couldn't—she refused to—think about that now. She didn't want to cry. Not in front of Travis. Not in front of anyone.

"How did you run that fast?" Travis asked.

Stevie ignored him. She didn't want to deal with Travis's questions—or her own—about the dream. It *had* to have been a dream. A dream of running with horses. No one could keep up with a galloping horse.

She forced herself to let go of the post and limped back to the house, each painful step insisting the dream had to have been more than a dream. She clenched her jaw against the pain and refused to admit anything. It was a dream. She had stumbled and fallen and that was it.

Travis walked beside her, saying nothing, until she reached the front porch. Then he said good-bye and left, walking away down the long driveway. She didn't watch him. She went into the house.

Chapter 3
A Peace Offering

STEVIE'S ANKLE IMPROVED over the afternoon, after a shower and sitting still while unpacking, her leg held straight in front of her on her bed. But her ankle still made her take the stairs down to supper very slowly.

"Are you going to take all night, Stevie?" Dad called from the dining room.

Stevie made herself stand up straight at the foot of the stairs. "Coming," she said. Then she forced herself to walk normally. After two painful steps, she settled for limping as little she could.

Half of the long dining room table had been cleared, and three plates set. Dad and Blake had already taken their seats, leaving the seat farthest from the door for Stevie. She suppressed a groan, and tried not to limp too noticeably around to her place.

Both of the men had started eating. Dad looked up at her as she sat down. "What happened to you?" he asked.

Now Blake looked at her. "Wow. What did happen to you?"

Stevie looked down at her plate. "Nothing," she said. "Is this Hamburger Helper?"

"Of course," Blake said. "It's Saturday. Did you and Travis get into a fight?"

"No!" Stevie said.

"Was he here again?" Dad asked, looking at Blake.

"I saw him walking down the driveway," Blake said.

Dad looked back at Stevie. "What did Travis want?" An unexpected edge in Dad's voice made Stevie risk a quick look at him. His face showed nothing. Dad met her gaze, waiting.

Stevie shrugged. "He didn't say." She used her fork to scoop a mouthful of creamy noodles and ground beef. She didn't notice the taste, just chewed, hoping that maybe having her mouth full would stop the questions.

It didn't stop Blake. "So he found you?" he asked around his food.

Stevie nodded, chewing with as much jaw movement as seemed reasonable. Obviously, her mouth was full. She couldn't answer questions with her mouth full.

"So what happened?" Blake asked. "You came in here looking like you got stampeded. Limping around, bruise on your forehead, and on your arm. And... is that blood on your shirt?"

Without swallowing, Stevie shoved another fork full of food into her mouth, then looked down at her shirt. After her shower, she had intentionally put on a t-shirt instead of a tank top to hide the scrapes on her left shoulder. She had been worried about the bruise on her right elbow, but she knew that a long sleeve shirt would generate even more questions. Besides, that bruise, like the one on her forehead, seemed to be getting better. Both had shrunk over the course of the afternoon. She had hoped that if she didn't mention them, no one else would.

Of course, Blake *would* notice.

She saw a few drying spots of blood on where her shirt covered her left shoulder. She chewed even more vigorously than before, so she wouldn't say, "Crap!" over and over again. Hopefully the blood would come out in the wash. It wasn't her favorite t-shirt, but April had given it to her, and she looked cute in it.

"What the hell, Stevie?" Dad asked. "What happened?" He paused, but went on before Stevie could swallow and respond. "Did you try to ride Jack Rabbit bareback?"

"I was just—" Stevie started. But the second question had to be answered first. "No," she said. "I didn't. I wasn't riding. I was..." What? What had happened? She had tried not to think about it all afternoon. Now she wished she had least thought up an explanation to give to Dad. "I was running," she said finally. "And I fell."

"Running?" Dad had his fork halfway to his mouth. Now it stopped. "Why were you running?"

Her mind raced, hoping she would have something to useful to say when her mouth opened. "I was... I was just happy to be home." Dad just looked at her, fork still in his hand, but resting it on the edge of his plate. Waiting for her to go on. She swallowed. "I ran with... to... to the pasture. I just wanted to see the horses. And I tripped," she finished. "That's all. I tripped. I didn't think it was that big a deal..."

Dad's eyes went to the bruise on her forehead, then to the blood on her shoulder, then to the bruise on her elbow. A tally of her visible injuries. Finally, his eyes came back to hers. "Not even back a *day*," he said. "Boys visiting. You getting hurt. Maybe you should've stayed in Tulsa, since you don't know how to act around horses anymore."

Stevie opened her mouth to respond, but the unfairness of Dad's words overwhelmed her. *Maybe you should've stayed in Tulsa.* She closed her mouth in shock. But then opened it again. "It wasn't... I didn't want to *go* to Tulsa," she said, her voice rising.

"Watch your tone," Dad said. "You know you had to go. There was too much going on—"

"You didn't have to send me away," Stevie almost shouted.

Dad glared at her, the muscles of his jaw clenching. Then he broke eye contact and resumed eating. Stevie just stared at him, unsure how to continue.

"You do need to be more careful, Stevie," Blake said, his voice low.

Stevie stared at Blake. Him too? Even Blake? "I know how to act—"

"Maybe you should stay away from the horses," Dad said, still not looking at her. His voice was no louder than before, but it stopped her. "Unless I'm... or Blake... is with you."

Stevie stared at both of them, her mouth open. Stay away from the horses? She closed her mouth then, and felt her face getting warm, felt a stinging in her eyes. "That's so... I just *tripped*," she managed to say, forcing the words through the tightening in her throat.

Dad made a noise, but didn't otherwise respond. He didn't even look at her.

Nobody said anything more after that, the only sounds those of the forks tapping against the plates, chewing, breathing. Stevie wanted to ask Dad—plead with him, if necessary—not to restrict her from the horses. But she kept her mouth shut. Dad hadn't actually said she had to stay away from the horses. He had merely brought up the possibility. *Maybe*, he had said. But the possibility scared her. Being home, at the ranch, without being able to ride— It was unthinkable. But if she didn't bring it up, maybe he would forget. Or just watch her closely. She would have to be careful the next day or two.

She wanted to talk to Blake about her training and which races they could make it to, but Blake looked pre-occupied, as well. Like there was something he wanted to talk about, but was also avoiding.

Or maybe, Stevie thought, Blake was just thinking about Shannon. Blake with a girlfriend. The idea still turned her stomach.

Blake caught Stevie's eye, and offered her a smile. Stevie resisted the urge to stick her tongue out at him, and continued eating.

Stevie finished what was on her plate, got up without a word, and took the plate and fork to the sink.

"Stevie," Blake said as she passed through the dining room again.

She started to protest that she didn't want to do the dishes, not on her first night home, but stopped herself.

"I'll be in my room," she said, and limped upstairs.

"You in there?" Blake asked, his voice muffled on the other side of Stevie's closed door. "Still feeling sorry for yourself?"

Stevie didn't answer. She sat on her bed, right leg stretched out in front of her, not reading the book she held open in front of her. She had picked up the book from the stack beside her bed, after *not* slamming her door and *not* throwing herself on her bed. She couldn't remember if the book was *Black Beauty* or *The Black Stallion*. All she remembered was the word "black."

"Can I come in?" Blake asked.

She thought about telling him to go away. Instead she said, "It's open."

The door opened enough for Blake to put his head in. His eyes swept the room, came back to her. "What you reading?"

"I don't know," Stevie said. She closed the book and put it on her nightstand, covering the still unopened birthday card. "Didn't you have plans for tonight?"

Blake seemed to hesitate.

"What?" she asked.

"You didn't change your shirt?"

Stevie blinked. That wasn't what she expected. She shrugged. "Why bother? Just get another one bloody. Why all the questions?"

"It's only six thirty," Blake said. "And I thought..."

He paused, waiting for Stevie to jump on the obvious bait. But she resisted. After everything that had happened today, she wasn't feeling playful.

Blake pushed the door the rest of the way open, and leaned against the door frame. "I'm sorry, Stevie. I didn't know Dad would take it that way."

Stevie looked away. "He didn't actually say—"

"He did," Blake said. "After you left."

Stevie sat up straight, outrage and horror rising in her chest. "That's not *fair*—"

"Wait," Blake said. He used his low voice again. The way he did when he was trying to keep people from yelling at each other, or at him. The way he did when he wanted her to listen.

She bit down on the long list of why it wasn't fair, why Dad had no *right*, why— Blake looked at her, waiting. She crossed her arms and looked back at him. "OK," she said. "I'm listening."

"He told me to make sure you stayed away from the horses unless either he or I was with you." Blake held up his hand, forestalling her outrage once again. "And I talked him out of it. So don't worry about it."

"That's so—" Stevie stopped and stared. Outrage became astonishment. Her arms uncrossed on their own. She leaned forward. "You talked Dad out of it?"

Blake shrugged. "He listens to me more these days." A shadow seemed to fall on his face then, and he looked away. "About most things," he added. Before Stevie could ask what he meant, he went on, "Anyway, it's only six-thirty." His eyes jumped to the digital clock on her nightstand. "Six thirty-five now," he amended. "And I wondered if you wanted to go out."

Stevie smirked. "What about your plans? Did Shannon get busy?"

Blake rolled his eyes. "No, stupid. I told Shannon I'd be taking my little sister out tonight."

Stevie lips pulled into a smile she couldn't stop. Take *that*, Miss Shannon Girlfriend. "Really?"

"Really. Did you want to change your shirt? Butcher's closes at seven. If you hurry, we can get there before then."

Butcher's! Stevie's smile became a huge grin. New boots!

She glanced at the dried spots of blood on her t-shirt, then decided she didn't care. She pushed herself to the edge of the bed and stood slowly. Her right ankle twinged, but hurt less now than before. Hurt less than her scuffed right knee now. "I'm ready," she said.

"Good," said Blake. "We need to get you some new shit-kickers. Because there's a lot of shit that needs kicking around this place."

"And riding boots," Stevie said, following him.

"Of course," he said.

Stevie wiggled her toes and relished the snug fit of her shiny new black roper boots. She wore them out of Butcher's Boots and Work Shoes, walking in such a way to make the heels and soles tap against the tiled floor. The concrete of the sidewalk didn't sound quite as impressive, but she kept it up. She didn't have to limp. Wrapped tight in fresh, aromatic leather, even her ankle felt better.

She carried the box with her new brown work boots, which would all too soon lose their newness and become full-fledged "shitkickers." She'd be wearing those boots almost all summer. Her ropers, though, she would only wear when riding. They needed breaking in. So, yeah, *of course*, she wore them out of the store.

Behind her, Blake said good night to Dan Butcher, and thanked him for staying open. "I should've known she'd want to try on every pair in her size," Blake added.

Stevie spun around in her new boots, showing off and only too happy to point out that a perfect fit—and the right cut and style—were important. She struck a pose, no explanation required.

Dan Butcher laughed and said it was nothing. "Not like there was a football game on I might be missing. And I'll always stay open for a sale."

Stevie walked to where Blake had parked Dad's truck. When she asked Blake about his own truck, the Chevy, he had shrugged and said he sold it. Stevie suspected Shannon had something to do with that, since Blake loved his beater of a pickup and drove it everywhere. But Blake had only chuckled and shook his head when she offered that theory.

Stepping down from the curb to the street reminded her ankle that it hurt, so she propped herself against the door to wait for Blake to unlock it from the inside.

Blake surprised her by coming around to the passenger side of the truck with her. He carried the box for the boots she wore, currently holding her sneakers. He motioned her out of the way and opened the door while she stared at him. Opening the door for her? Was he crazy? Had Shannon already broken his will?

"You think you can walk a couple blocks in those?" he asked. He tossed the box with her sneakers into truck.

"Sure," Stevie said. Her ankle ached in protest, but she ignored it, happy. She had her Blake back. She could put up with a little joint pain. She put the box with her work boots into the truck. She stepped back while Blake shut the door. "Where we going?"

"This way," Blake said, and led her across the street. "I figured we could get a cherry limeade."

"Sonic!" Stevie said. She followed him, all pains and grievances forgotten, heels and toes tapping on the asphalt of the city street.

"They should hear us coming," Blake said. "All that racket."

Stevie stomped the next few steps extra loud for his benefit, then laughed. "I'm just happy," she said. "New boots. Two new boots," she added. "That's never happened before."

"Happy belated birthday," Blake said. "For the ropers, anyway. Dad gave me the money to buy the work boots. Can't have you lounging around all summer when there's work to be done."

Stevie grinned, almost hearing Dad saying exactly that. And she decided that maybe Shannon hadn't broken Blake after all, if he still had money left over to spend on his little sister. "Thanks!" she said. "So does that mean you're going to help me race?"

"Of course," he said. "But we'll talk about that more in a minute."

They weaved through the Saturday night drag traffic to the Sonic Drive In. They sat at one of the picnic tables between the two rows of parking bays and ordered their drinks from a girl that Stevie remembered had played basketball for the high school team. While they waited, a truck pulled into one of the nearby bays and honked. They both waved at the man and woman in the truck, Mike and Linda Reilly. Then the door of a car opened and a girl got out, shouting, "Stevie!"

Stevie spun around on the picnic bench—so that her new boots were on display—and waved. "Hey, Michelle."

Michelle Young walked over and Stevie stood up so they could hug each other. "I'm so glad you're back," Michelle said. Then she added, "For the summer, at least."

"I'm back to stay," Stevie said. She threw a glance over her shoulder at Blake. "At least, no one's told me any different."

Blake didn't meet her eye, watching cars pass by on Main Street.

"Nice boots," Michelle said, then poked Stevie's shoulder with a finger—the right shoulder fortunately. "You didn't call me."

"Blake just bought them for me," Stevie replied. "And I just got back."

"Hi, Blake," Michelle said, with a quick smile and finger wave. Then she looked at Stevie again. "You just got back? I thought you were coming in on Thursday?"

"I was," Stevie said. "But..." She paused. Some details didn't need to be shared. "Well, it took a couple extra days."

"I guess so." Michelle gave her another hug. "It's good to see you. We were about to go, but I saw you and I wanted to run over and welcome you back."

"Who are you here with?" Stevie asked, looking past Michelle back at the car.

"Oh, just my brother," Michelle said. "But he wants to go—before too many people see he's out with his sister. Call me, OK? Tomorrow?"

"I will."

Stevie sat down as Michelle ran to the car, which started moving before she got there. Stevie's and Blake's drinks had arrived. Blake was sipping his through the straw, a look of supreme patience on his face.

"Shut up," Stevie said. "She wasn't here *that* long. And she barely looked at you. How did that happen?" Michelle had had a crush on Blake since... well... forever.

Blake shrugged. "Maybe she outgrew me. Or maybe she's got a boyfriend now." He reached into his back pocket then and pulled out a folded piece of paper.

"Boyfriend?" Stevie asked. How long had it been since she talked to Michelle? Spring break? Christmas? Surely not that long.

Blake just shrugged. He unfolded the paper and spread it before him on the table.

"Tell me what you know," she said.

"I'm sure I don't know anything," he said, his too-smug smile flashing for an instant.

Stevie started to pull the straw out of her drink, loaded, the straw squeaking against the plastic lid of the cup.

"Don't even think about it," Blake said. "And," he added, the look of longsuffering patience coming back, "I thought you wanted to talk about racing..."

Stevie forgot about Michelle as she recognized the contents of the creased paper Blake had open in front of him. "That's my list." She pushed the straw back into place and reached for the paper. "What have you circled?"

Blake smacked her hand, and she drew it back. "Hold on a minute," he said.

Stevie held her offended hand and tried to look hurt. It was hard, since she also wanted to grin like a fool.

"I told you this morning that I would do what I could to help you this summer," he said. "And I will. But," he added, "you have to understand that I can't... *you* can't... go to a race every week."

Now it wasn't hard to look hurt, but Stevie kept her mouth closed. Blake wasn't finished talking.

He pushed the paper toward her. "I've circled the races I'm sure we can make."

Stevie snatched up the paper and scanned down the list of events she had so carefully planned. Blake had circled four of them. "Just four?"

"The first one is in three weeks," Blake said. "June 23rd, in Hugo."

"Three weeks?"

"You haven't done much riding this past year," Blake went on, ignoring her question.

He didn't mention that Jack Rabbit had thrown her. But Stevie heard that in his pause. She started to say, again, that it wasn't as if she hadn't been thrown before, and she had already gotten back in the saddle, and she would be more careful—and so would Jack Rabbit. But Blake went on.

"You're going to need to practice," he said. "Just about every spare minute between now and then. And there aren't a lot of spare minutes available."

Stevie looked at the list again. "What about the weekend before July 4th?"

"Shannon and I have plans that weekend."

She looked up. "What kind of plans?" Not that she cared. Not really. But it was costing her a race.

"The next one is in mid-July, in McAlester," he went on, ignoring her for the umpteenth time. "That's a pretty big event, and should be a lot of fun. Dad will probably want to come to that one too."

"And Shannon?"

"Maybe," he said. "And there are two races in August. The first one I can take you to, like the others, the one in Durant."

Stevie returned her attention to the list, visualizing a calendar, and wishing the summer didn't seem so short when she looked at it this way.

"You'll have to convince Dad to take you to the one in Muskogee," Blake added. "I think I'll be able to get there and watch, but I won't be able to drive you."

"Why not?" Stevie asked, not looking up from the list. The two races in August were three weeks apart, the second one might be after school started. If it involved missing school, Dad would be a hard sell.

"Because I won't be here."

Now Stevie looked up. "You won't be where?"

"Here," Blake said, gesturing around him. "The ranch. Antlers. Southeast Oklahoma."

"You're moving away?" Stevie asked, pulling back from the table and Blake. And away from the idea of ever leaving Antlers. "Why? Where? Is it Shannon?"

"No," he said, shaking his head. "It's not Shannon. I'm going to O.S.U," he added, smiling and looking proud of himself. "I'll be starting classes that week. I'm pretty sure," he added, picking up on Stevie's horrified expression, "I can bum a ride from Stillwater to Muskogee to see you race, though."

Stevie just stared at him. "You're leaving?"

"I'm not *leaving*," he said. "I'm going to college. To Oklahoma State University."

"That's even further away than Tulsa. How can you go that far away? I just got *home*, and now you tell me you're leaving?"

Now Blake looked hurt. "I'm not leaving *today*. Classes don't start until the third week of August. I was hoping you'd be happy for me. I wasn't sure I'd be accepted. But I was."

Stevie opened her mouth, then closed it again. She wanted to be happy for Blake. But she had just got home. To what was left of her family. And now it was getting even smaller.

"It's not like I'll be gone forever," Blake said. "I'll be back for Thanksgiving and Christmas—"

Stevie had heard that schedule before. "Dad's going to send me back to Tulsa for sure." The look on Blake's face made her wish she hadn't said it. But once the thought had occurred to her, she couldn't shake it. Dad had sent her to live with Aunt Mary and Uncle Rick after Edwin's funeral. He would send her away again if Blake left. She just knew it.

"You don't know that," Blake said.

Stevie just looked at him. Like he was blind. Or crazy. Or both.

He sighed. "Yeah, you're right. But look, we can work on that too. Maybe..." His voice drifted off and looked away.

Any hope seemed worth latching onto. "Maybe what?"

"Maybe," he said again. "Maybe things will change, and Dad won't have to do that." Blake shook his head. "Let's not talk about that right now." He reached across the table and put his hand on hers. "Be happy for me, Stevie."

Stevie wanted to pull her hand back. And she wanted to grab onto his hand with both of hers and hold him there, prevent him from leaving. She had just spent ten months wishing every night that she could be home. Mom was long gone. Edwin had been taken away. And now Blake was leaving.

Blake looked at her and she wanted to smile for him, but she couldn't. "Why?" she asked.

"Because this is what I want," he replied. "This is what I've been looking forward to for a long time."

"You want to leave us?" Stevie tried to take her hand away, but he held onto it.

"You know that's not it," he said. "You and Dad are all the family I have left. And it's going to be hard to be away from you both. And the ranch," he added.

"And the horses?"

"Them too," he said. "Though I doubt I'll miss having to feed them every morning. Or cleaning out their stalls. Or mowing their pastures."

"What are you going to do?" she asked. "Study, I mean. Are you going to learn more about horses? Or ranching? At college?"

Blake laughed. "No. I'm going into engineering. Maybe architecture."

He continued talking, telling Stevie about the courses he had signed up for in the fall semester. She watched him talk, using both of his hands, the colorful neon lights flashing in his eyes. Stevie gave him a weak smile and nodded where it seemed appropriate. But she wasn't listening. Not really. She tried to understand, because it was obviously what Blake wanted to do. Still...

Horses and riding were her life. All she'd ever known, all she'd ever wanted to do. Like Blake—and like Edwin—she had grown up on the horse ranch, in Antlers. Except for the last school year, she had lived in Antlers her entire life. She couldn't imagine wanting to move away, even for a short time. And four years didn't seem like a short time, at all. And architecture didn't sound like something Blake would be coming back to Antlers to do.

"Anyway," Blake said, "I don't want to bore you with too many of the details—"

"Too late," Stevie said.

Blake rolled his eyes. "Should've known. Besides that, though, I want you to know that I'll do everything I can to make sure you can race those four times."

"Everything you can do? Or just what Shannon *lets* you do?"

Blake laughed, but didn't say anything. He just laughed.

"What?" Stevie asked.

"You're so jealous," he said. "It's cute."

"I am *not* jealous."

Blake chuckled again. "If you say so. Grab your drink. It's time we headed home." He stood.

"I'm not jealous," Stevie repeated. Blake laughed and walked away from the table, making her run to catch up with him. She barely noticed her ankle.

Chapter 4
More Bad News

STEVIE LOOKED AT her forehead in the mirror and poked the small spot of bruise that remained. She winced. The bruise might be smaller this morning, but it still hurt. The bruise on her right elbow looked much the same way. And the scrape on her shoulder seemed to be healing quickly, as well. White scar tissue had formed under the scabs, contrasting with the tanned color of her skin.

Her ankle still hurt. She had noticed that when she walked barefoot from her bedroom to the bathroom. The good news seemed to be that the pain had been reduced to a dull ache.

Much like the dull ache that permeated the muscles of her arms and legs. She felt like she had run... for miles, at least. Like the day after she had to run laps in PE for expressing her real opinion about the coach and the coach's two class pets, Kelly Nichols and Amber Coffee. How many laps had she managed to run in those thirty minutes of class time? She didn't remember. Too many. And all the next day—and the day after—her legs had felt like they were about to fall off.

Today felt just like that. Except her arms felt it too. And when she yawned, she felt other muscles complain, muscles in her back and chest that she had never known she had.

A hot shower helped. Some.

She pulled on her jeans and a tank top, and stomped her feet into the new work boots—new boots wouldn't break in themselves—and learned of still more aches. She wondered if this was what it felt like to be old, with everything aching and not being able to make it stop, just hoping it would get better.

So far, the only positive thing she could think of about the morning and waking up was that the sun on her closed Venetian blinds indicated it was ten in the morning. The digital clock on her nightstand confirmed her hunch.

Neither Blake nor Dad had come to wake her. They had let her sleep in. Sunday's had always been late starting days on the Buckbee Ranch. A tradition Stevie remembered every weekend for ten months. Because Aunt Mary and Uncle Rick were regular churchgoers. And they never even considered leaving Stevie home to sleep in on a Sunday.

She had no doubt, though, that the early mornings would start up the next day. Monday morning, bright and early.

And probably achy, she thought with a frown as she stretched again.

Then Stevie wondered if Dad and Blake had forgotten about her, forgotten she was home. Maybe her sitting at the dining room table and eating breakfast would come as a shock to them. Wouldn't that be funny?

No, she decided. Not funny at all.

She had been gone too long. And it looked like she might be gone again when school started in August. She didn't want to spend another year in Tulsa, away from her friends, away from Blake—except he was going to be gone, even if she wasn't—away from Dad, away from her horses. At least she had riding and the races—only four of them, true, but that was better than she had begun to think was possible. At least she had those to look forward to. The summer hadn't gotten off to a very good start, but maybe it was still salvageable.

Maybe she would even be able to ride some today.

Thinking about how she would roll the practice barrels from the big barn to the practice pen after breakfast, she started downstairs. The heels of her boots thumped on the hardwood stairs, but didn't stop her from hearing Dad and Blake talking—shouting at each other—in the office.

"—aren't you at least willing to think about it?" Blake's voice, loud. "The agent told me that just based on the acreage alone—"

Stevie paused halfway down the stairs, aching muscles and practice barrels forgotten. Agent? What kind of agent?

"No!" Dad's voice, just as loud. "We are not going to talk about this."

Stevie took another step, softly now, not letting the boots make any noise.

"We have to talk about it, Dad. I'm going to be gone, and you can't afford—"

"Don't tell me what I can and can't afford, Blake. Or what I can and can't do. Don't tell me what burdens I can and can't carry. I've been carrying this ranch, this family, for longer—"

"Dad, you have to—" Blake was trying to get himself under control, Stevie could hear it in his voice. But Dad didn't seem to care.

"No!" Dad shouted. "I don't have to do anything. And I will not sell. This ranch was our dream. Mine and your Mom's—"

Stevie clung to the banister as the force of the words pushed past her, and the meaning of the words, and the argument, hit her. Sell the ranch? How could they even be talking about that? How could Blake be trying to talk Dad into it?

"Mom is *gone*, Dad." Blake's voice was calmer now, but more biting, harsh.

"—and it was *my* dream," Dad plowed on, with no attempt to control himself, his voice booming through the house. "Even before it was hers. And I'm not going to give it up. Even if she has. Even if you have."

A long moment of silence. Then Blake spoke again. "You've already given up."

"Is that right, Blake?" Now it was Dad's voice that had the bite, and a hint of a sneer. "Then why am I going to be the last one here? After you've run off with your girlfriend. Isn't that what you're doing, Blake? Giving up? Quitting? Running away? From me, from Stevie—"

"No, Dad. I'm—"

"From everything?"

"No, Dad. I'm not—"

"Just go," Dad said. "Go. I'm not talking about this anymore."

"Dad—"

"Go!"

"—you have to listen to me!"

"GO!" Dad was almost screaming now.

Stevie cowered on the stairs, still clinging to the banister, fighting the urge to start bawling. She watched Blake stomp out of the office and push his way through the front door, off the porch, into the morning sunshine. He didn't look back, didn't notice her on the stairs, stuck, unsure of where to go or what to do. Or how to feel.

The old wood of the fence groaned in protest as Stevie climbed and perched on the top rung, the heels of her boots hooked on the next lower rung. From there, she could see the horses grazing.

The horses had been left in the southeast pasture overnight, taking advantage of the weather. Rain and Buckaroo and a few of the others nickered at her when she arrived. The rest bobbed their heads then continued grazing and swishing.

Rain looked at Stevie and seemed to be inviting her to join the horses. Stevie smiled and waved, but remained on the fence. She hadn't thought to grab any carrots. And she had skipped the kitchen entirely, skipping breakfast after watching Dad stalk from the office to the kitchen—like Blake, he had not seen her on the stairs—and so she hadn't picked up any sugar cubes.

At least the sun had warmed her on her walk from the house, soothing some of the ache in her arms and legs, and taking the edge off the cold sick feeling in her stomach.

She didn't know what to think about Blake trying to convince Dad to sell the farm. So she didn't think about it. Much.

She tried to focus on her plans. Jack Rabbit hadn't been trained for barrel racing, so he would require a lot of work. Both she and he would require a lot of practice. Rain had been a barrel racing horse, and wouldn't need as much re-training. But Rain had been Mom's horse, and thinking about Mom meant remembering the birthday cards that reminded her year after year that Mom had left. And that Blake would be leaving at the end of the summer. And that Blake was trying to convince Dad to sell the farm.

She didn't want to think about any of that.

Rain blew out loud enough to be heard even though the horse stood at least fifty yards away with Buckaroo and Hobo and Scamper. Stevie looked at Rain but her gaze didn't linger. Her eyes looked past the horses, to the line of trees around the ranch.

She wanted to train with multiple horses, at least at first, while she was getting her riding skills back. Spread the burden of her lack of practice. Buckaroo had also received some barrel racing training, a few years ago, from his previous owner. He might be a good alternative to Rain. Younger.

Stevie thought she heard another snort from Rain, but didn't look over.

From the corner of her eye, she spied movement. She turned her head to see Travis Delozier walking toward her from the direction of the house. He nodded a greeting when she looked at him. He wore a battered ball cap today, the bill casting a shadow across his face. She thought she could see his brown eyes in the shadow, though.

"Hey, Stevie," he said as he got closer. He said her name like a normal person. Not the way Edwin always said it, drawing it out to *Steeevie*. The way Edwin *used* to say it.

Stevie remembered the... what? vision? ghost? she didn't know... of Edwin she had seen yesterday. She didn't know what to think of that either. Yesterday had too many mysteries. Combined with the argument between Dad and Blake today, it had re-opened too many old boxes of memories she had thought closed and put away.

"You OK?" Travis asked.

Stevie realized she had just been watching him walk up, saying nothing. She hadn't really been *seeing* him, though. She remembered thinking about his brown eyes, and she felt her face get warm. "Yeah," she said, looking back at the horses. "Hey. Travis," she added, feeling unusual as she said his name. Saying it normal, like he had said hers. She almost asked him when the two of them had become friends. Or at least normal with each other.

But he spoke first. "Is your ankle OK?"

She nodded, still looking away. "Mostly. Twinges a little."

"That's all? It twinges?" Travis stepped up to the fence and leaned against it, looking up at her. "I thought you might be on crutches today."

"God, no. I mean, thank god, no." Aunt Mary had always gotten onto her about saying "god." As if everyone else didn't say "god" the same way Stevie did. But still, even if Aunt Mary was a long drive away, today was a Sunday. "Dad wouldn't let me come *near* a horse if..." Her voice trailed off.

Dad had almost done that, anyway, crutches or no. But Blake talked Dad out of it. *He listens to me more these days,* Blake had said last night. *About most things.* Stevie now understood one of the things Dad didn't want to listen to

Blake about. She didn't want Dad to listen to Blake about selling. She didn't want Blake to talk about it. Not to Dad. Not to her. Not to anyone.

"How was Tulsa?"

Stevie shrugged. She was still too caught up in the drama of Blake and Dad fighting to want to talk about Tulsa. It was too far away to matter. And too close for comfort. Either way, it just didn't seem important. Tulsa was Tulsa. It wasn't home, and she didn't want it to ever be home.

"So are you," Travis started, then stopped. After a few seconds, he asked, "Are you going to run with the horses today?"

Stevie looked at him. She extended her right leg. First the tired muscles protested, then her ankle complained when she flexed it, despite the support of the new boot. She grimaced in pain and let the leg bend back to where it had been.

"I guess it's too soon," Travis said. "After yesterday. And probably hard to run in boots, anyway." He turned his head, looking at the horses, the brim of his hat blocking her from seeing his eyes.

Since he couldn't see that she was still looking at him, Stevie kept looking at him, wondering.

What had he seen yesterday? Had he really been at the fence when she saw Edwin? Or had she imagined him there too? Had he seen her run? He had obviously seen her fall. If she had really run with the horses, what had she looked like?

She wondered why he was here, talking to her. Did he like her? As in *like her* like her? He had never indicated anything of that nature that before. Travis was Edwin's friend. Over at the ranch all the time, except when he and Edwin were at the Delozier house. Almost like another brother. Almost. She might've had a crush on him at one time, years ago, but she had outgrown it, and him. She had only been six then, or seven. Too young to know better. She still liked him, of course, but not *that* way. And he was two years older. There was no way he liked her, even if she liked him back. A freshman liking a seventh grader? It was almost unthinkable.

She turned back to watch the horses. She wondered if Travis knew that Blake was going to OSU. Probably. Probably everyone in Antlers knew by now. She would have been the last one to know.

Her mind came back to an earlier question.

"Why are—" she started to ask Travis.

"Do you think—" Travis started to ask her at the same time.

They both stopped.

"What?" Stevie asked after a long minute of silence.

"It's not—" Travis said, then cut himself off. "What were you going to ask?"

Stevie shrugged. Her question suddenly seemed too forward, too suggestive. Or maybe a bit rude. If she asked him why he was there, he might go away. She didn't want him to go away. "Nothing really."

She sat on the fence, and he leaned against it, neither speaking for another long minute, both of them watching the horses swish and flick and graze in a leisurely fashion. Stevie noticed that Rain still kept an eye on her.

"Are you going to race this year?" Travis asked.

Stevie looked down at him, saw he was looking up at her again. "Is that what you were going to ask?"

Travis shrugged. "Barrel racing, right?"

Stevie nodded. "Yeah. Blake—and Dad—are going to help me train," she said, "and take me to the races." She paused, realizing that he had been going to ask her something else. It was obvious. She could see it in his face. But then she went on. "Four of them."

"Where at?" Travis asked.

Whatever he had been going to ask, racing was something Stevie had been wanting to talk about for weeks. She adjusted her seat, swinging her right leg over so she straddled the fence. The old wood squeaked as she did that, and wobbled a bit, but continued to hold her. Travis raised

a hand to the fence, as if to steady it, or her. Stevie continued, "I had wanted to go to more races, one a week, some in
Texas, some in Arkansas, the rest in Oklahoma..."

Once started, finally able to talk about her plans for the
summer with someone, she kept going. Even if those plans
had been changed, that only gave her more reason to talk
about them. To compare her plans with what, she hoped,
could still happen. Travis looked at her as she talked,
nodding at the proper points, asking questions when she
waited for them, and looking at the horses as she talked
about Jack Rabbit and Rain and Buckaroo.

She didn't remember Travis being more than passing
interested in horses or riding before. She had seen him
ride, and he rode well, but she knew it wasn't something he
lived for, like she did. Still, he listened as she talked.

She turned the rest of the way around on top of the
fence, facing him, with both hands free now to gesture. She
told him about coming home, and— "Blake told me you had
come by on Friday," she said.

Travis had been leaning against the fence, his shoulder
pressed against the top beam, the one she sat on. Now he
stood up straight, his eyes leaving her face and drifting to
the empty southwest field.

Stevie stared at him. She had never seen Travis look...
what? Shy? Had she embarrassed him? She leaned forward,
looking closer.

"What—"

The loud squeal of old metal rubbing against old wood
cut her off as the fence beam gave way. She fell forward. The
ground came at her fast, and in that brief instant wondered
how her right ankle would take this new stress of impact.
Dad was going to be so upset—

But she—somehow—collided with Travis first. She fell
against his left arm as his hands closed on her waist and
held her away from the ground. She had only just begun to
realize what happened when he set her down lightly. The
fence board hit the ground with a thump behind her.

She faced the fence now, spun around in her fall, with Travis between her and the fence. He released her, and her legs managed to hold her up. Her breathing, though, seemed to be shallow, and her heart raced. From the near fall.

Then she saw the fence board slanting down to the ground. "Oh, that's just great."

Travis seemed about to say something, but he followed her eyes and stepped out of the way.

The end of the board she had been sitting on rested on the ground. The other end was still nailed to the fence, but only just. Both fence posts still stood upright, so the fence hadn't totally collapsed, and none of the other cross beams on this section had been affected. She looked at the nearest portions of the fence, noticing for the first time how old the wood looked. Even the big wooden gate.

Rain stood on the opposite side of the fence. She gave a concerned sounding nicker.

"I'm alright, girl," Stevie replied.

The horse lifted her right foreleg, curling it up. Then she stamped it to the ground, raising a small dust cloud.

"No," Stevie said, answering the obvious question. "My ankle is fine. Travis caught me."

"Who are you talking to?" Travis asked. He looked at her, then at Rain.

Stevie just shook her head.

After a second, Travis chuckled and said, "That's twice in two days."

Stevie looked at him. "What?"

He flashed a smile. "It's just not your week," he said. "You've only been home two days, and you've already gotten hurt—or almost hurt—"

Stevie glared at him, and blew air out her nose. She remembered Blake teasing her last night, at dinner. *You look like you got stampeded.* And Dad. *Maybe you should've stayed in Tulsa, since you don't know how to act around horses anymore.*

"Just shut up," she said, to her memories, and to Travis, her voice harsh.

Her anger startled him. "What? I just—"

"Just help me prop this back up," Stevie said. She squatted and picked up the end of the board. "Hold that end against the post," she said. Travis did as he was told. "Make sure it doesn't come loose. Maybe I can..."

Together, they put the fence beam back up, pushing the bent nails back into their holes. The beam held, but Stevie knew it wouldn't last. And a broken fence was dangerous with horses around.

"I better tell Dad about this," she said. With that, she turned her back on Travis and headed back to the house. She wondered if Travis would follow her, then she decided she didn't care. Because even he thought she had forgotten how to act around horses.

Dad, Blake, and now Travis. Nobody believed in her. But she would show them, her and Jack Rabbit both. Behind her, in the southeast pasture, she heard Jack Rabbit whinny agreement.

Chapter 5
Just Like Your Mother

STEVIE DIALED MICHELLE'S number, her hand shaking but her fingers finding and pushing the buttons from long, if neglected, practice. She pressed the cordless phone to her ear only slightly harder than necessary and listened to the ringing. She took a deep breath and let it out.

She sat on the front porch. Over the railing, lit by the afternoon sun, she could see the northern half of the Buckbee Horse Ranch, from just inside the main gate, past the northwest pasture and the practice pen to the big barn, and from there to the empty corral and the tractor barn and the nearest of the northeast pastures.

The corral was empty now. Only one horse was visible, standing near the gate connecting the corral to the north pasture. Stevie knew which horse it was, and refused to look at her.

Stevie focused on the ringing again, to drown out the memory of Rain's words, and closed her eyes, not wanting to see the blemishes of the ranch all around her. The weeds, the spots of rust, the bent and broken fence wires, the old and splintering wood. She forced herself to remember the way the ranch had looked all her life. Until now.

A man's voice answered on the other end. "Yeah?"

"Bryan?" Stevie said. Her voice cracked, just the tiniest bit, from the strain. She had just taken the second shower of the day, cooling down after being in the sun for hours, calming down after everything that had happened, but the tension was still there. She cleared her throat, covering the lapse, and said more clearly, "Hey, Bryan. Is Michelle there?"

"Yeah, hang on." Then, muffled, Stevie heard him shout, "Shelly! Phone." Then the sound of the phone being put down on a hard surface.

In her excitement to be home, she hadn't seen any of problems. Or if she saw them, she hadn't noticed, seeing only isolated issues—like the fence she broke and went to tell Dad about—and not the problems those blemishes and scars added up to.

Walking back to the house, though, leaving Travis and Rain standing there on opposite sides of the broken fence, she had begun to see, as if her eyes were finally opened. Weeds ran along the fence lines. Potholes marred the twin ruts of the gravel driveway that led from the gate to the parking area bounded by the big barn, the corral and the house, and more weeds sprouted in the middle. The tall grass of the lawn that circled the house showed the lawn hadn't been mowed in weeks. And she saw the broken fence wires of the practice pen that would have to be fixed before she could safely ride there.

She tried not to think about the problems. Any of the problems. About Blake and Dad. About them arguing over her and the ranch. She refused to think about Blake moving away. About Dad drinking more than ever before. And about Rain—

No. She wouldn't think about that either.

"This is Michelle."

"Hey," Stevie said, back in the present, at least enough to talk. "Your dad still calls you Shelly?"

"Stevie!" Michelle's voice warmed up, reverting from the adult sounding tone she had answered with to the girl

Stevie had known all her life. "Yeah, Dad's still living in the past, bless his heart. I've been telling him and telling him—"

"Telling me what?" Stevie heard Bryan Hunter ask in the background.

"That my name is Michelle, you dork," Michelle replied, her voice muffled. "Remember? The name you gave me?" Then she was back. "What are you doing later?"

"Nothing," Stevie said. "Just..." *Just sitting on the porch while my Dad finishes the day's bottle of scotch in the office.* No, there was no reason to say that to Michelle. Or anyone else. "Nothing," she said again. "You going out?"

A bottle of scotch and an empty glass had been an integral part of Dad's desk in the office for as long as Stevie could remember. The faint smell of the drink on Dad's breath never bothered her—though the smell of the scotch still in the bottle or in his glass always made her wrinkle her nose in disgust. So did the taste.

Blake had given her some once, just a splash in the bottom of a plastic cup, years ago. Her and Edwin both, actually. "Teaching them a lesson," nine year old Blake had called it, explaining to Dad why Stevie and Edwin had thrown up in the office, all over the hardwood floor. Dad had taught Blake a lesson then, before teaching Edwin and Stevie as well. Stevie had never been tempted by the scotch before then, and had decided that night she would never even think about drinking it again.

Blake once told her that he could remember a time when Dad's desk didn't have the bottle and the glass. A time before Mom left. Stevie, with no memories of Mom that didn't have matching photographs, hadn't believed him. But she had been jealous. She still was. Some. Even if it was Mom that had screwed up her life. And Dad's. And was still screwing it up.

"We're going to watch a movie," Michelle said. "Mom and Dad and me. Did you want to come along?"

"Yeah," she said. She didn't say, *Take me anywhere—anywhere but here.* She added, "That'd be great."

"What's up? You sound down."

Stevie smiled. The two of them had been getting in trouble for talking in class as far back as K-4, and for staying up all night talking at sleepovers for just as long. Talking was what they did. But Stevie wouldn't tell her friend everything. Not about this. She just needed... what? A friendly voice. Someone who didn't think she was—

"I'm just tired," she said, cutting off the thought. "Getting unpacked and all."

"Yeah, I'm sure that's tiring. A movie is just what you need, I think, after a long move. What do you want to see?"

"I have no idea what's even showing," Stevie said. "Remember? I just got back? I'm sure whatever's showing—"

"Hang on," Michelle said. "I'll get the— No, wait. Curtis," she shouted, her voice muffled again. "What's showing at the Phoenix?"

"Michelle," Stevie said, trying to get her friend's attention.

"I'm not taking you to the Phoenix." Curtis's voice, faint, as if from another room in the house.

"I didn't say you were, butthead," Michelle said. "I just asked what was showing."

"Michelle," Stevie said again. "It's not important. Anything is fine."

"Oh, OK," Michelle said. Curtis's voice rumbled in the background, but Stevie couldn't make out the words. "Piss off," Michelle said. "We don't care anymore." More of Curtis's voice, and Michelle squealed into Stevie's ear. "Go *away*," she shouted. Then, "Dad! Curtis is being a pain in the butt."

"Dad," Stevie had called out earlier, pushing into the house. "There's a section of fence broken in the southeast pasture."

Dad sat at his desk, looking out the double windows at the ranch. He didn't respond.

Stevie watched his eyes fall to the empty glass on his desk, watched his hand reach out and pick up the bottle. He took off the stopper and poured a small amount into the empty glass, covering the bottom, re-stoppered the bottle and put it down again.

Over spring break, confined to the couch in the living room across from Dad's office, Stevie had heard him, and watched him, do that time after time. When Dad came into the house between chores, to check on her. And, having checked on her, sitting down to have a drink. She barely noticed, though. Because Dad had always done that. She tried not to think that he did it more often now. She told herself it was just because she had been there, in the house, day after day. So she saw it more.

"Dad," Stevie said again.

Dad picked up the glass, but paused with it almost to his lips. His head turned and he looked at her. "What?" he said. "I thought you were..." He shrugged. "Out. You sneaked out."

"I didn't sneak out. Not really. I was at the southeast pasture. A board came off the fence by the gate."

Dad turned his head to look out the window again. "Tell Blake," he said. "Not that it'll do any good," he added before Stevie could respond. "He's been damn near worthless ever since he got that letter from the college." He downed the drink in one gulp. He grimaced and gave a light gasp.

The attack on Blake shocked her. So did Dad just sitting there. "But, Dad," she said, stepping closer. "The horses are in that pasture."

"I told you. Go tell Blake. If you can find him. If he hasn't left already."

Stevie bit her lip, unsure. She stared at Dad's profile. He just sat there. Not getting up, like she expected—like he should have done—to move the horses out of the southeast pasture.

"Go," Dad told her again, and dismissed her with a vague shooing gesture.

This was wrong. "But the horses—"

"The horses will be fine," Dad said, overriding her. "Just go tell Blake. Or do it yourself."

Stevie stood there for a long second. First Blake, wanting to sell the ranch. Now Dad, just sitting there, sending her after her brother when the ranch needed attention. "Where is he?"

Dad turned to look at her again. She met his eyes, trying to look into them, to see what he was thinking. But his eyes told her nothing.

"Dad?" she said. "Where is—"

"I expect you'll leave next," Dad said.

"—Blake? What?" Stevie stared. This was not at all what she expected. She looked back at the front door, wondering where she was. This couldn't be her home. She felt her forehead get tense as she looked back at Dad. "Why would I leave?"

Dad shrugged. "Why does anyone leave? They grow up. They get tired of feeding horses, and taking care of them and all their crap. They get sick of shoveling shit and fixing fences."

The office, the entire house, seemed to spin around Stevie as Dad talked, his calm, level voice belying the confusion that assaulted her. Stevie squeezed her eyes closed and shook her head to clear it. She couldn't believe it was Dad telling her this, any of this. Dad, whose entire life revolved around his ranch. And his horses. And, she had thought, around herself and Blake and Edwin.

"Or they die," Dad added, as if reading her mind. "So, yeah, I expect you'll be the next to go—"

Sudden fear and tears pushed behind Stevie's eyes and tightened her throat. She thought of Tulsa, and tried to control her emotions. "Are you going to send me away?" she asked, interrupting Dad.

He stopped talking for a second, then continued. "You're just like your mother. Always thinking about yourself. And you're going to run off and leave me. Just like she did."

Stevie's mouth opened but she had no idea what to say. Only a hoarse sob came out, and she lost control of her tears. She reached out a hand to Dad, wanting him to reach for her and pull her to him and tell her that he hadn't meant any of it. Tell her that he wouldn't send her away, not to Tulsa or anywhere else. Tell her that she wasn't anything like her mother.

But Dad just looked at her, unmoved and unmoving, watching her cry.

She wanted to rush to him, but his eyes kept her away. She lost her balance under the pressure of his stare, took a step backward.

"See?" Dad said. "I told you." He looked away now. "I saw you out there," he went on. "With Travis Delozier." He paused, as if waiting for Stevie to deny it. "He took Edwin." For the first time, Stevie heard emotion in Dad's voice, a bitterness. "And now he's going to take you."

Stevie's hands shook and her legs felt like they would collapse. Her eyes still gushed tears and her mouth could only open and close. No words made it past the tightness in her throat. No words seemed to have any meaning, not if Dad could say such things.

"Dad?" she managed to force out of her chest. She wanted to say, *Dad, it's me, Stevie.* But all that came out was another, "Dad?"

"Go," Dad said again, not looking at her. He picked up the bottle, and pulled out the stopper.

Stevie turned around, not wanting to see him pour the scotch, or put the stopper back in the bottle. Or pick up the glass and down the drink. She heard the sounds, though, the splash, the clink of the stopper.

She forced her legs to move, to carry her out of the office. She ran to the glass door and leaned against it as she fumbled for the latch, refusing to hear Dad's intake of breath, the cup returning to the table. She pushed the door open and stumbled onto the porch, taking in a huge breath, as if she had been suffocating. She held onto one of the porch posts and waited for the world to stop spinning around her.

She sobbed and the tears continued to pool in her eyes and run down her cheeks, warm even when touched by the morning breeze.

"I'm not," she managed to say, telling the ranch, the sky, the world—everyone and everything but the one person she wanted to tell it to most. "I'm *not* like Mom." The tightness in her chest eased as she said it. So she said it again. "I'm not like Mom." She took another deep breath, and let it out slow. "I'm not. And," she added, feeling the strength return to her legs and arms so that she could let go of the post and stand on her own. "And I'm not going to leave."

She resisted the urge to look over her shoulder, to see if Dad was watching her. She wished he was. She really did. So she imagined him sitting there, looking at her, impressed that she stood on her own. She knew he hadn't heard her, but she imagined that too, and that he agreed with her.

She used both hands to push the tears from her eyes. She needed to find Blake, so they could move the horses. And she didn't want him to see her crying.

"Are you there?" Michelle's voice. "Stevie?"

Stevie pressed the phone harder against her ear, almost painful, so that she could concentrate. "Yeah," she said. What had Michelle been talking about? Latonya Cummings? Or was that earlier? She remembered something about Travis Delozier, but she wasn't sure if Michelle had said it, or if Dad's words had hit her again. "Sorry. What were you saying?"

Michelle laughed. "You really are out of it. I said that Latonya said that she's seen Travis Delozier walking over to your ranch a lot this week."

"Oh, yeah," Stevie said. "He's... stopped by."

"To see you?" Michelle asked, prompting, pumping.

"I'm not sure." A week ago—or even yesterday—the question and the implication would've made Stevie's face go green. Now, though... she didn't know. *He likes you.* Rain's words, repeated in her head. Stevie pushed the words away, and thoughts of Rain with them. "He... he didn't say."

"Uh huh," Michelle said. "So not much change there. But what did he *do* while he was there?" she asked, hinting at scandal. "And what did *you* do?"

Stevie ignored the innuendo. "He helped me," she said. "With the horses," she added before Michelle's imagination got too creative. "A fence broke, and we had to move the horses."

She didn't find Blake. The truck remained where Blake had parked it the night before. But Stevie didn't find him in the big barn or the tractor barn. Blake had walked away from the ranch.

Stevie sighed, and realized that she was going to have to walk the horses back to the corral by herself. She could figure out where to move them after that. Or someone could. She wasn't sure she should be making decisions like that. Except no one else was offering to make them for her.

She went back to the big barn and grabbed a halter and lead rope. It would take forever, leading the horses one by one, but she didn't have any choice.

"What's the matter?"

Still on edge, still tense, still shaking on the inside and trying not to cry—*I'm not like Mom!*—Travis's voice surprised her. Her heart pounded in her chest and she almost cried out. She almost fell apart, collapsing into quaking pieces there on the floor of the barn.

But she didn't. She caught herself, held herself together, and made herself look at Travis.

"I'm not," she started, but stopped before she could finish the protest. "I have to get the horses back to the corral."

Travis looked at her. The shadows of the barn hid her face. She hoped. She could see his face. He looked... concerned? For her?

"Do you need a hand?"

Stevie nodded, and held out the halter and lead she carried. Travis took them, then waited while she got another pair for herself, then they walked back to the big gate of the southeast pasture.

Jack Rabbit stood by the broken fence, watching them walk up. Behind Jack Rabbit stood Satchmo and the other geldings, looking at Jack Rabbit. The fence beam had fallen again, Stevie saw, both sides having come free now, and it lay in the grass at the foot of the fence. Or maybe it hadn't fallen.

Jack Rabbit turned his face away from her at that thought.

Like a movie in her mind, Stevie saw Jack Rabbit—not from her own perspective, but as if she stood in the pasture. She saw Jack Rabbit leaning against the weakened fence until the loose end of the beam fell as it had before. And then pushing against the other end of the beam, where it was still connected to the fence post. He had to push harder on that one, but the weakened nails finally gave way and the whole top portion of the wooden fence had been removed. Jack Rabbit whinnying, proud of himself, then falling quiet as two people came from the house.

The sight of herself, walking with Travis, made Stevie's head hurt and stung her eyes. She blinked.

When she looked at Jack Rabbit again, he still wouldn't meet her gaze. Her eyes met those of Satchmo behind him.

The blue roan didn't like Jack Rabbit.

Stevie's eyes grew wide, and *something* pounded in her head. Not an image and not words. Just an emotion. From Satchmo, about Jack Rabbit.

Jack Rabbit snorted, and drew Stevie's attention. He looked her in the eye this time. With a gesture of his head, he took credit for the fallen fence beam. And when he bared his teeth, Stevie knew that Jack Rabbit didn't think much of Satchmo either.

The pain in Stevie's head made her stop walking. She rubbed her temples, as much as she could without dropping the halter and lead rope.

"Are you OK?" Travis asked.

"No," Stevie said, squeezing her eyes shut, trying to block the visions of herself and Travis that bombarded her from all sides, all different angles. She even saw herself with her head in her hands, eyes closed. She could see Travis, looking at her, one hand reaching as if to help her but held back by uncertainty. Her head felt like it would burst.

"I'm not— I'm not OK," she went on. "Almost nothing is OK. So please stop asking me that."

The pounding in her head faded, and she opened her eyes. Rain now stood beside Jack Rabbit, but none of the other horses had moved. They all seemed to be looking at her.

"Stevie?" Travis said. He looked from her to the horses.

"Shush," Stevie said, trying to prevent the headache coming back. "Just be quiet."

Travis closed his mouth.

Stevie took a deep breath and let it out slowly. She didn't know what was going on, but she knew how to act around horses. And she knew how to take care of them.

"OK," she said. "You get Satchmo. No. Get Scamper this time, then Satchmo. I'll get Jack Rabbit." She needed to get Jack Rabbit to the corral before he tried to jump the fence. And Satchmo too, but she didn't want to leave the two of them alone in the corral. This would have to do.

Jack Rabbit walked right up to her when she opened the gate. The big horse managed to keep his back to Satchmo as he did, and stood there, head high, exuding pride at being first.

"Good boy," Stevie said. Even though she had to reach up on tiptoe to get the halter over his head. She didn't wait for Travis to get Scamper—she knew he could do it. She led Jack Rabbit through the gate and to the corral.

She and Travis walked back and forth, from pasture to corral. They passed each other going opposite directions, or held the gates for each other, or closed the gates behind each other as they needed to. But they didn't talk. Sometimes Travis looked like he wanted to say something, but his eyes would meet hers and he would stay silent. It took them two hours to get all twenty-four horses into the corral.

Stevie left Rain for last. Because the mare would behave herself. Because Rain kept watching her, as if the horse were responsible for the girl. And because looking at Rain reminded her of Mom.

When Stevie came for Rain at last, the horse stood by the gate of the pasture, waiting. Rain dropped her head so that Stevie could slip the halter on.

"Good girl," Stevie said, and stroked Rain's neck.

None of the horses had made it difficult for either Stevie or Travis. The horses had remained near the gate, instead of moving out into the pasture. And none of them had seemed to resent the halter or the lead as they were walked to the corral. So the task hadn't been as hard as Stevie feared. Still, it was a lot of walking, especially in new boots with a sore ankle—and a lingering, on again off again headache—so she felt grateful to Rain for ducking down and making it easy.

She led Rain out of the pasture, pulling the gate closed for the last time.

Twenty-four horses. The number kept returning to Stevie. She couldn't remember when the ranch had had so few horses. From fifty-six last summer, to twenty-four now. The ranch had lost two-thirds of its boarders. How had that happened?

"Where did everyone go?" Stevie said out loud as they walked, casting a glance at Rain.

A rush of images hit Stevie between the eyes. A succession of memories, of days and nights and seasons and faces of horses and men and women and trucks and trailers with ramps and wide open doors pushed into Stevie's mind. She stood in a pasture—all the pastures—while the herd thinned around her, familiar scents of friends fading into memory, stalls in the barn empty and lifeless, the man— Stevie saw Dad's face—drawing away, the first boy—now Stevie saw Blake—distracted, the second boy—Edwin, with Travis—gone, and the child—her own face, but younger, still a child—no longer around. A growing sense of age as the world changed, as horses—and people—came and changed and left.

Stevie stared at Rain, and Rain looked back at her. Stevie swallowed, unsure—about everything. She realized she had stopped walking, and started again, though she was still looking at Rain.

Another impression came into her mind then. A thought of Dad. Stevie looked forward, and saw Dad coming out of the barn. He carried a length of wood on his shoulder, the ten-foot painted fence beam extending out in front of him and behind him. He had his tool belt on, with the hammer hanging from it. The handle of the hammer knocked against his leg as he walked toward Stevie and Rain.

Dad met Stevie's eye as they passed one another, but he only gave her a short nod, a glimmer of approval. And maybe a hint of an apology. Maybe.

He looked so alone that Stevie wanted to reach out to him, hug him, and make sure he knew that she still loved him and needed him. And that she missed Edwin too. And Mom.

But Dad remained at a distance, even as he walked past her.

"Don't leave them in the corral," Dad said. "Open the gate to the north pasture."

Stevie bit her lip to stop the tears from coming back. "OK," she managed to say, though she wasn't sure she said it loud enough for Dad to hear.

Travis waited for her at the gate to the corral and opened it for her as she walked woodenly beside Rain. She had Rain step around until the horse faced the gate, then took off the lead and halter.

Stevie stood there, looking at Rain, and Rain looked at her. She heard the gate close behind her, but she didn't move.

You're a lot like her. A woman's voice, in her head. The same voice she had heard yesterday, welcoming her home.

Her hands shook and she looked at Rain.

"Who—" she started. *Who am I like?* she wanted to ask. Or, *Who is talking?* But she stopped herself. Because how could she be asking Rain this question? Or any question at all? And because she was scared of the answers.

Ever since she got home—no, before that, from that first, long, disappointing day of waiting in Tulsa for Dad to come get her—and even before that, going back to the night that Dad stood in front of her, then held her close while he told her that Edwin was dead—she seemed to be in some kind of dream. Or nightmare.

She just wanted to wake up and have everything back the way it was. Before Edwin died. Before Mom—

Your mother, Rain said—it had to be Rain—the voice again in Stevie's head. *You're just like her. Pretty, smart, good with horses—*

"No," Stevie said, shaking her head and backing away. The betrayal was too complete, and cut too deep. Even her horses. She turned her back on Rain and walked away. *I'm nothing like Mom,* she wanted to say, but she only ground her teeth together, refusing to say anything.

Travis smiled at her as he moved to opened the gate for her. She met his eyes, but didn't return the smile. She pushed the gate open, out of his grasp, and walked away, leaving it for him to close.

She felt—something—brush against her mind, and the memory of the smell of Rain's mane came to her. And another memory, of hearing a voice—Rain's voice—in her head as she cried herself to sleep. She tried to close her mind, push Rain out of her head.

"Stevie?" Travis's voice, behind her, uncertain.

"Open the gate to the north pasture," she said, still walking away. She didn't hear if Travis responded.

He likes you. Rain's voice, fainter now as Stevie continued to put distance between them and tried not to hear or feel. *The boy*, Rain added. Stevie couldn't see the horse, but somehow she knew exactly who Rain meant. Travis Delozier. *Though maybe not the way he thinks.*

Stevie shook her head, saying no to the all the words she couldn't shake. *You're just like your mother.* Dad's words. *Your mother. You're just like her.* Rain's words. Over and over.

"No," she said, whispering through her tight throat. "I'm not. I'm not like her at all." She said it each time the voices in her head insisted otherwise.

She went into the house, up to her room, repeating the denial. Wishing she could wake up and her life would go back to the way it had been.

"It's too late, Stevie." Michelle's voice, in her ear. "There's no going back."

"What?" Stevie asked, confused and lost, trying to figure out what was dream, what was nightmare, and what was real.

"Travis, silly. It's too late. The rumors have already started."

Stevie sighed. "I just don't understand."

"What's to understand?" Michelle asked. "Maybe he always liked you, and just hung out with Edwin to be close to you."

Michelle's teasing almost made Stevie smile. But she decided they had talked enough about Travis. "When are you going to go to the movie?"

"Don't try to change the subject," Michelle said, then added, "Mom and Doofus are getting ready. So I guess I better do that too. We'll be there in a few minutes."

"I'll be here," Stevie said. "Sitting on the porch."

"We'll honk from the gate," Michelle said.

Stevie put down the phone, and looked over the porch railing, at the fading ranch and the overgrown driveway and the darkening sky, everywhere but at the horse who stood near the corral, just inside the north pasture, looking at her.

Chapter 6
Stevie Rides

"I'M SORRY, STEVIE."

In her dream, Dad held her close, a hand on the back of her head, stroking her hair, like he used to do when she needed comforting. "Things will be back to normal," he said. "Soon."

Then they stood in the practice pen, and Dad held Jack Rabbit's reins while Stevie mounted. The practice pen became an open field, with the sunlight washing over them—

"Stevie." A man's voice, but not Dad's.

The sunlight disappeared, darkness enveloped her. Then the sun flashed on again. Off again.

"Stevie, get up."

Stevie opened her eyes. Early morning gray lit the room. Someone stood at her door.

She propped herself up on an elbow. "Dad?"

The someone at the door flicked the light switch and the gray became bright, penetrating incandescence.

Stevie's eyes shut on their own, and she turned her face so that the light no longer hit her face. "What?" she asked.

"Are you awake this time?" Not Dad. She could tell that now. Though it did sound a lot like him. Blake.

"What time is it?" She squinted against the bright light and tried to focus on Blake at the door of her room.

"The clock on the wall says..." Blake paused. "Five o'clock."

"Five?" Stevie thought she recognized a song in Blake's tone of voice, but it was too early to be playing "name that tune." "Why are you waking me up at five?"

Blake settled into his normal slouch against her doorframe. "Two reasons," he said. "Or maybe three."

Stevie let herself settle back into her pillow and closed her eyes.

"Don't go back to sleep."

"No promises," Stevie said. After a long pause, Blake still hadn't said anything. She opened one eye to see if he was still at the door. He was. "Well?"

Blake sighed. "I'm sorry," he said.

"For waking me?" Her voice was husky. She thought about clearing her throat, but decided she liked how grumpy she sounded.

"No. For not being around yesterday. For leaving you with... for leaving you alone here."

"I wasn't alone," Stevie said. "Dad was here..." Her voice trailed off. She cleared her throat now, to cover the tightness of her voice.

Blake nodded. "Yeah."

Stevie closed her open eye and turned over so that her back was to Blake. Blake still hadn't been home when she got back from the movie with Michelle. Dad had been there, of course. Sitting on the porch swing, though, instead of in his office. He didn't have his glass with him, but he hadn't met Stevie's eyes. He glanced at her when she sat down on the porch swing beside him, and then looked away. After a few minutes, he put his arm around her shoulders. They didn't talk. Stevie didn't know how long they sat there in the last light of a bad day, not talking. The only words said were, "Good night."

Stevie opened her eyes to stop the memories playing back behind her eyelids. She looked at a blank spot on the far wall as she kept her back to Blake. She wasn't mad at him. Not really. But he *had* abandoned her. He should've been home. Not out with Shannon. Or wherever he was. She almost asked if he had been out with Shannon, but decided she didn't want to know. And Blake would probably call her jealous again. And she so wasn't.

"I'm sorry," Blake said again. "I should've been here."

"It's OK," she said. And it almost was. Or would be soon. She couldn't stay mad at Blake for long.

"Did you have to move the horses by yourself?"

"Travis helped me."

"What do you think about Travis?" Blake asked.

Stevie turned over and stared at Blake. "What?" *He likes you*, Rain had said—somehow—among other things she seemed to have said, as well. Things Stevie refused to think about. Unless Stevie was going crazy and had imagined the whole thing, and Rain's voice in her head was another part of the bad dream. Of course, Michelle had brought up Travis over and over last night. Now Blake.

But Blake wasn't even looking at her. He was looking past her, through the Venetian blinds, out at the ranch. "I was just thinking," he said. "We have to get the ranch back in shape. And if he's going to be here, anyway..." He looked at Stevie, and winked.

Stevie groaned and pulled the blankets over her head.

Blake laughed.

From under the blankets, she asked, "Are you finished? Can I go back to sleep yet?"

"Not a chance, baby sister."

She heard him move and tried to get a better grip on the blankets, but they pulled out of her hands as he yanked them from the foot of the bed.

He smiled down at her. "Rise and shine."

Stevie grabbed her pillow and threw it at him as he ran out of the room. The pillow missed, landing on the floor outside her door, where Blake had dropped her top sheet and blanket.

* * *

"You ready to ride?" Blake asked Stevie.

"We didn't get the practice pen fixed," Stevie said. She had been fretting about that all day. Blake assigned her one chore after the other, throughout the day, but they never came close to the practice pen. First she mowed the lawn close to the house and the lanes of grass along the driveway, then used the hedge trimmers to cut down the biggest weeds by the fences that the mower couldn't reach. That had taken most of the morning. Then, after lunch both she and Blake started cleaning out the stalls in the barn. After several hours of that, making only a dent in the work required, they sat in the air-conditioned tack room and cleaned and treated the bits and halters and saddles.

"There's more to riding than racing," Blake said. "And if you're finally finished with that saddle, bring it with you."

"Done," Stevie said, tossing the polishing cloth on the workbench.

Blake picked up a saddle by the pommel, slung it over a shoulder, and grabbed two bridles from the hook on the wall. "Then let's go pick us some horses to ride before dinner."

Stevie stood up and grabbed her saddle. Every muscle in her body protested at once, but they cooperated with her demands and she lifted the saddle. She ignored the aches and the weight of the saddle and followed Blake out of the tack room, and through the barn and into the open air of the corral. Blake lifted his saddle onto the top of the fence, then did the same with Stevie's.

"I don't have to guess which horse you want to bring in to ride," Blake said as they walked into the north pasture a few minutes later, each of them carrying halters and leads. "But... well, can I talk you into riding Rain? Or even Buckaroo?"

"Why? What's wrong with Jack Rabbit?"

Blake shook his head. "Nothing's wrong with him," he said. "He's the healthiest damn— He's the healthiest horse on the ranch. But I've only saddled him up and ridden him a few times since you... since spring break."

Stevie's excitement at riding dimmed, just a bit. Apprehension, then irritation, flitted through her mind at being reminded yet again. The scar on her lip tingled. "I'll be fine," she said. "And Jack Rabbit too. We'll both be fine." Her voice sounded sharper than she intended, so she laughed to cover it. "I only got kicked by a horse," she added. "I'm still a Buckbee."

Blake looked at her, and gave her a chuckle. "Should've known that thick head of yours—"

Stevie's boot heel came down on his toe.

"Oww!" he said, louder than was probably necessary, then reached to grab her, but she squealed a laugh and skipped away from him.

The horses turned to look at the two of them. Stevie still laughed at Blake, trailing behind her with an exaggerated limp, both of them walking again to avoid spooking the horses. Being with Blake, feeling the joy of being outside, smelling the scents of the pasture and the horses, all of it reminded her of running among the horses. And she felt the urge to run, to show Blake what she could do—

But what if it had all been a dream?

As she had worked on the day's mundane chores, the unbelievable events of the weekend had seemed to recede, to become more dreamlike. Like another part of the movie she had watched with Michelle the night before, all special effects and make believe. Because how much of it could have been real? Running with horses? Understanding horses? Seeing through the eyes of horses? *Talking* to horses?

Even less believable was that Dad would sit in his office when the horses needed him. Or that he would tell Stevie—

Except that part came with enough pain to assure Stevie it had been real. The wounds in her soul were still fresh, still painful.

Dad hadn't been up yet, so Stevie and Blake had eaten breakfast by themselves. She had wanted to ask Blake about Dad then—Dad had never gotten up later than Stevie at any time that she could remember—and throughout the day. But she didn't know how. When she would start to ask Blake, she couldn't. Blake had noticed, but if he sensed what her unspoken question was about—or who it was about—he never offered any response.

You're just like your mother. Dad's voice still rang in her ears. The two-cycle roar of the lawn mower had not been enough to drown out those words. She had denied it, silently, with every weed she had pulled up or chopped down, with every shovel full of old straw and manure she had scraped out of a stall. Dad was wrong. And she would prove it.

It wasn't a dream. The woman's voice interrupted Stevie's thoughts, and she found herself face to face with Rain. *And being like your mother—*

Stevie thoughts evaporated into pure anger. She looked in Rain's eye and tried to block out Rain's words. The force of her anger felt like a heavy door slamming shut in her mind, cutting off Rain's voice.

The horse pulled her head away in surprise, even taking a couple steps back from Stevie.

Stevie felt something brush against her mind, a tentative touch, Rain reaching out to her. But Stevie didn't respond. She held her anger and her bitterness—*I am not like my mother!* she almost shouted it—like a wall between herself and the horse. They looked at each other for several long heartbeats, then Stevie walked around Rain to where Jack Rabbit stood.

Jack Rabbit nodded at her as she walked up. He kept his head high again as she reached up with the halter.

"This would be a lot simpler," she said, "if you would just drop your head a bit."

The horse nickered, laughing at her, and held his pose for a few more seconds. Then he dropped his head. Some. Stevie still had to stretch to the get the halter on his head, but at least she didn't have to go on tiptoes or jump. Or use the stool Blake had brought for her.

"Good boy," she said. Her hand went automatically to her pocket, but she hadn't thought to grab a carrot or a sugar cube before walking out of the barn with Blake. "Sorry, boy. I'll get you a treat when we get to the barn."

Jack Rabbit accepted her apology—but only if she made good in a few minutes.

Stevie laughed, then looked around to see which horse Blake had chosen. She frowned as she saw him almost a hundred feet away trying to sweet talk Satchmo into standing still. The blue roan, though, just kept snorting and shaking his head. When Blake stepped closer, Satchmo stepped back.

"What are you doing?" Stevie asked, almost having to shout. "Satchmo and Jack Rabbit don't like each other."

"You think I don't know that?" Blake said in the same calm tones he had been using with Satchmo, Stevie barely hearing him across the pasture. He smiled his heart melting smile. "Come on, Satchmo. It's all good. It's your turn today. You know you'll like it." His hand went to his back pocket then and came out with a carrot. "Here you go, boy. All yours."

Jack Rabbit looked at the carrot in Blake's hand, then swung his head to face Stevie again. The accusation was obvious.

"I said I'm sorry. I forgot."

Jack Rabbit snorted, and pulled against the lead rope.

"Calm down," Stevie said, tightening her grip on the rope and pulling out some of the slack. "I said I would get you one." When she looked over at Blake again, he had the halter on Satchmo's head now. As they walked toward where Stevie and Jack Rabbit waited, Satchmo crunched on the carrot loudly enough to be heard across the pasture.

"The way Rain walked up to you," Blake said, "I figured you would change your mind."

"I won't change my mind," Stevie said.

"I think you might've hurt her feelings. Look at her."

Stevie turned to look at Rain, who stood to the side, watching them walk back to the corral. Even through her shield of anger, Stevie could feel the mare's regret and distress. "Good," Stevie said. Beside her, Jack Rabbit champed agreement.

"Good?" Blake said. "What's that supposed to mean?"

"Nothing." She looked away from Rain.

Blake looked at her, but Stevie didn't meet his eyes.

Under the awning of the turn-in Blake took the lead rope from Stevie. "I'll tie them up. You go get the curry brushes and the blankets."

The sound of a shovel scraping against the floor told Stevie that Dad was in the barn, continuing the work she and Blake had started earlier. She hesitated just inside the door, suddenly reluctant to face Dad. Despite sitting together on the porch the night before, as if everything was fine— Because it wasn't fine. What would he say? What would she say? They had seen each other only at a distance all day, never close enough to talk.

She forced herself to start walking again. She looked into the open stall doors as she walked down the aisle to the tack room.

Dad looked up as she passed. He met her eye and gave her a quick nod, then went back to work.

The air conditioning in the tack room was colder than she remembered, sending goosebumps down her arm. She grabbed the curry brushes and pulled two saddle blankets off the rack. Even the blankets seemed cold when she draped them over her shoulder.

"Stevie," Dad said as she came out of the tack room.

Stevie's heart skipped, surprised. Dad stood at the front of the stall he was cleaning. He wore his typical work clothes, sweat stained t-shirt and faded blue jeans pushed into the tops of his work boots. His stomach strained at the cloth of the t-shirt where he had it tucked into his jeans. Stevie almost stared. When had Dad developed a paunch?

"Tell Blake I want the whole barn cleaned by Friday," Dad said.

Stevie nodded. "OK," she managed to say. When Dad didn't turn away, she added, "We're... we're taking Jack Rabbit and Satchmo out for a ride."

Dad pointed to the stall across from where he was. "You cleaned those, right?" He didn't wait for Stevie's nod. "Do a better job tomorrow." Dad turned then and went back to scraping out the stall.

Stevie bit her lip, wanting to say more, wanting to talk to Dad. But she didn't know what to say to his back. After a minute, she walked past him out to the turn-in. She passed on Dad's message to Blake, who just nodded.

They didn't talk to each other as they curried the two horses. Both Jack Rabbit and Satchmo remained skittish, despite the low-voiced assurances of Stevie and Blake.

Jack Rabbit nodded when Stevie thought that Blake should've picked another horse. She heard Satchmo nicker, voicing his agreement as well. She didn't hear a voice in her head, or voices. Instead, images bombarded her from two sides, like disjointed, competing movie clips. The messages jumbled together, pounded together in her mind, but seemed to express the same thing. The horses wanted her to know that they both thought highly of her and Blake, it was the presence of the other horse involved that they resented—

"Stop!" Stevie said, almost shouting. She moved the curry brush to her left hand and pressed the palm of her right hand against her forehead, hoping to keep her brains from squeezing out of her skull.

"What's the matter?" Blake's voice, very close. She felt his hand on her shoulder, trying to turn her to face him.

She didn't shake off his hand, but she didn't let him turn her either. "Headache," she said. For several long, painful seconds, the images—Jack Rabbit rearing, Satchmo stamping the earth, challenges, responses—kept hitting her, slamming into her mind like the throbbing of a bruised thumb. She tried to remember how she had blocked Rain's voice before. She had been mad, and hurt. But she wasn't mad at Jack Rabbit, or at Satchmo. She just wanted them to *shut up* for a minute.

"That must be some headache," Blake said.

Stevie gave a short nod, not wanting to disturb the contents of her skull too much. Finally, the intensity of the images backed off. Jack Rabbit radiated surprise, and she felt Satchmo's concern behind her. She breathed easier, glad of Blake's hand on her shoulder, holding her up.

"Maybe we shouldn't—" Blake started.

"No," Stevie said. "I'm fine now. We're going to ride." She turned to look at Blake now, and uncertainty was obvious on his face. "I'm fine," she said again, telling all three of them: Blake, Jack Rabbit and Satchmo.

Stevie focused on her brush strokes after that, watching her hand with the brush move across Jack Rabbit's sleek coat, trying to keep at bay the headache that still lurked behind her eyes. She finished currying and spread the blanket over Jack Rabbit's back, pulling it to lay down the coat. Blake had to help her get the saddle onto the tall gelding. She tried, but almost dropped the saddle. Her tired muscles and the aftereffects of the headache combined to make her feel weak—almost useless.

Finally, reins in hand, she put her left foot in the stirrup, grabbed the pommel, and pulled herself up. Her right leg went over saddle and her foot found the stirrup on that side. She settled into the saddle. She kept the slack out of the reins to keep Jack Rabbit steady and patted the horse's neck. She looked over at Blake, who stood on the far side of Satchmo, watching her. She saw his eyes judging her foot in the stirrup and her hands on the reins. She caught his eye and grinned.

"I'm fine," she said. Then she laughed. "I feel *great*." And she did. The headache had disappeared, and she felt as if she were borrowing Jack Rabbit's strength in her arms and legs.

"Take him around the corral a couple times," Blake said. "I want to see how much you've forgotten."

Stevie laughed again. "I haven't forgotten *anything*. Let's show him, Jack Rabbit." Even as she formed the words, as her hands and legs shifted, giving the commands to the horse, Jack Rabbit turned to the right. The two of them walked, heads high, around the perimeter of the corral.

"Aren't we snooty today," Blake said as they came back around. "I think you're supposed to post if you're going to keep your noses that high in the air."

Stevie laughed. Satchmo blew out, letting Stevie know that Jack Rabbit was *always* snooty. Jack Rabbit maintained a dignified silence, not deigning to respond, making her laugh again.

"Now turn him and go the other way," Blake said.

Stevie and Jack Rabbit complied, still maintaining their stately pace and postures. With each step, Stevie felt the restrained power of Jack Rabbit's muscles, and she wished to let that power loose, to see what wonders they could perform together, girl and horse.

Satisfied that she hadn't become totally incompetent after her months away in Tulsa, Blake led Satchmo to the corral gate and opened it. Stevie and Jack Rabbit followed them out of the corral.

"Where we going?" Stevie asked. She looked down the driveway to the county road. She didn't expect to be let loose on a long, straight stretch of road, or even the well-worn dirt path beside the road. But she could hope.

"Southwest pasture," Blake replied. He still didn't mount, leading Satchmo across to the first gate to the south pastures. "We're going to have a bit of fun."

The southwest pasture wasn't quite as fun as a long trail ride, but it would be a nice substitute. Jack Rabbit picked up Stevie's excitement, and pranced as they walked.

"Steady," Blake said, looking up at Stevie. "Don't let him carry you away."

"That wasn't him," Stevie said. "That was me."

Blake looked at her like she had said something stupid. "Just keep him under control. He can be hard to manage. I

wish I had had more time to work with him this year, but..."
He stopped talking, and opened the next gate.

"But what?" Stevie asked as she and Jack Rabbit walked through the gate.

"Nothing," Blake said. "I just wish I'd had more time to work with him. He's got the makings of a first-class horse."

"Of course he does," Stevie said. Jack Rabbit agreed. Now it was Satchmo's turn to not respond.

They walked down the fenced path between the southeast and southwest pastures. Stevie could see the new fence beam Dad had put up yesterday. The fresh white paint of the beam looked out of place on the old, faded fence. Like a Band-Aid on unwashed skin.

"What happened to the fence?" Blake asked.

"It broke," Stevie said. Then she added, "Dad fixed it."

She couldn't read the expression on Blake's face. "What do you know about that?" he asked, looking at the fence.

"I was sitting on it," Stevie said, putting into her voice her lack of belief that he hadn't understood her the first time she said it. "It broke. Dad fixed it," she said again, feeling like she was defending Dad.

Blake looked at her, his expression still unreadable. Then he opened the gate to the southwest pasture. "Run around a bit. We'll catch up."

"Maybe you will," Stevie said, smiling. "And maybe you won't."

Just like in the corral, even as she thought about exploding through the gate, taking up the slack in the reins and lowering herself and tightening her grip with her legs, Jack Rabbit responded.

Like his namesake, Jack Rabbit bounded forward, front legs stretching out in front of him as his powerful back legs pushed against the earth. Or maybe the earth moved beneath them. Stevie couldn't be sure. In an instant they were through the gate and speeding along the fence.

Jack Rabbit's red mane leaped and flowed in time with the four-beat gait of his gallop, flashed like fire in the afternoon sun. Stevie felt her own hair whipping behind her. She imagined Blake still looking at the spot where she and Jack Rabbit had been a second before, surprised to see them vanish in a blur of speed. She laughed, the wind of their pace pulling the sounds and her breath away from her.

They didn't slow for the first corner of the pasture, taking it in a wide curve, as if they were on a race track, horse and rider leaning into the curve.

Through her hands on the reins, her feet in the stirrups, her legs holding onto Jack Rabbit's mid-section, Stevie felt herself becoming one with the horse. She and Jack Rabbit were a single creature now, moving in harmony, relying on each other, breathing in unison, muscles flexing and clenching and relaxing, hard hooves striking the ground, pulling the ground to them and pushing it away behind them.

The next corner of the pasture was carved out like the first, but even faster than before.

Stevie felt her weight on Jack Rabbit's back now, but knew that she wasn't a burden because she lent him the additional strength he needed to carry her. Together, they were one. He could carry her forever. They could run forever. If only the pasture extended that far.

Too soon the third corner of the pasture came at them, turning them back toward the center of the ranch, back toward Blake.

Blake hadn't even mounted yet, Stevie saw. He stood just inside the closed gate, Satchmo's reins held in his hand, watching her, surprise visible on his face even from this distance.

Stevie laughed again and adjusted Jack Rabbit's course so that they sped directly toward Blake and Satchmo. Jack Rabbit's gait stretched out and he pushed forward even faster than before. The burst of speed sent a rush to Stevie's head. Her heart beat in time with Jack Rabbit's heart and with his hooves striking the ground.

Jack Rabbit continued to dig deeper and push harder and Stevie watched Blake's surprise turn to shock and she felt her connection to Jack Rabbit begin to unravel.

They were going too fast.

Feeling the first knots of fear in her stomach, Stevie pulled back on the reins, and settled back into the saddle, but now Jack Rabbit didn't respond. He pulled against her, still trying to go even faster, and using her own strength against her.

They wouldn't be able to stop in time.

In front of them, the distance shrinking incredibly fast, Blake spun and grabbed hold of Satchmo's bridle to keep the horse from rearing.

Stevie pulled back harder now, separating herself from Jack Rabbit in her mind, reasserting her role as the rider in their partnership. It felt like trying to rein in a runaway freight train, but Jack Rabbit finally began to yield. She shifted his lead, forcing him to slow down and curve away from Blake and Satchmo, so that horse and girl passed right in front of them with only inches to spare.

She drew Jack Rabbit up and they spun around to face Blake. Stevie wanted to ask if Blake had seen that lead change. She couldn't remember when she had done it so well before, so naturally. But she bit her lip and said nothing when she saw the look on Blake's face.

Blake stood there, still holding Satchmo's bridle and stroking the roan's neck, trying to calm him down. Stevie could feel Satchmo's alarm, and could see it clearly in the horse's eyes and bared teeth. Blake kept his voice level and reassuring even as his eyes caught Stevie's and flashed anger, cutting off her apology before she could form it.

Stevie waited in silence. Jack Rabbit stood with his held high, oozing disdain for Satchmo. He tried to turn so his back was to Satchmo, but Stevie wouldn't let him. "Stop it, Jack Rabbit," she said, pulling him back around to face Blake and Satchmo.

Jack Rabbit snorted in disgust and turned his face to look to Stevie's right, as if he were interested in the pasture fence.

After a few minutes, Satchmo settled down and Blake stepped into the saddle. He pulled up alongside Stevie. Stevie met his eyes. Jack Rabbit still looked away.

"I sure as hell hope Dad didn't see that," Blake said. He shook his head. "You're a good rider, Stevie, but—" He stopped and seemed to be struggling with his own calm, even as Satchmo fidgeted beneath him. "Damn it, Stevie, you've could've seriously hurt both horses. Not to mention you and me."

"I knew what I was doing—"

"No!" Blake said. Satchmo, picking up on his rider's anger, pulled away from Stevie. Blake brought the horse back around so that his face was close to Stevie's again.

"You lost control of the horse," Blake said. "You were playing around like some kind of god damn *tourist*, and you almost—" He stopped again, but Stevie could see the words he was sparing her in his eyes. She couldn't remember the last time he had been this angry with her.

He was right, but Stevie wasn't ready to admit that yet. "But did you see—"

"Stop," Blake said. "Just stop."

Stevie stopped, biting down on the words hard enough to rattle her teeth.

"Come on," Blake said, and started Satchmo forward. "Just ride alongside. Don't talk," he added when she took a breath to do exactly that. "Let's just ride and calm down."

Stevie let out her breath. She didn't think she—or Jack Rabbit—were the ones who needed to calm down, but she kept that to herself. Unlike before, Jack Rabbit didn't start forward with just a thought. Steve had to snap the reins and nudge his ribs with her heels to get him to walk alongside Satchmo.

Blake didn't look at her the entire first lap. Stevie sneaked glances at him, though, wondering how angry he really was. She saw the muscles of his jaw clenching and unclenching from the chewing out he wasn't yelling at her. She wanted to tell him that she hadn't lost control. There had been only that brief instant when Jack Rabbit resisted, and she had taken him in hand again. No one had been hurt. And she had never ridden so fast before. Protests and appeals she wanted to make. Except Blake wasn't accusing her. At least not out loud.

She felt worse than if he had yelled at her.

"I'm sorry," she said as they finished their second lap of walking around the perimeter of the pasture.

"I hope so," Blake said. He pushed Satchmo into a trot.

Stevie followed suit. Jack Rabbit pulled against her, wanting to go faster and get in front of Satchmo. Stevie didn't wait for the sideways glance from Blake to restrain Jack Rabbit, and let Satchmo keep his half-length lead. She and Jack Rabbit were in trouble. Even if Jack Rabbit didn't want to admit it.

Blake pulled up at the gate after the next lap. Stevie pulled up as well, hoping that the riding hadn't ended already. And on a such sour note.

"Show me that lead change again," Blake said. "Back and forth over there," he added, pointing to where he wanted Stevie to ride. "So I can see what you're doing." Then he smiled. "I want to see if you did it on purpose. Or if you just got lucky."

"Of course I did it on purpose," Stevie said.

But Jack Rabbit's mood hadn't improved yet, even if Blake's had. Stevie's first two attempts to demonstrate a lead change didn't have any effect on Jack Rabbit. He maintained his starting lead. She tried to remember how she had managed it. The change had felt so natural at the time, Jack Rabbit responding as if he was a part of her. He wasn't responding like a part of her now. And he forced her to be emphatic with her simple commands too, like trotting and reining in and even turning around.

Getting frustrated—with Blake's amused look as well as Jack Rabbit's resistance—Stevie focused on Jack Rabbit's shoulders as they trotted until she could feel the muscles and bones as if they were her own. And on her next try, as if Jack Rabbit's legs were her own, between beats, she extended her—his—left foreleg instead of the right one that Jack Rabbit had started with.

Jack Rabbit stumbled, but the lead change happened. The next time, going from left back to right, went smoother.

"You're doing it," Blake said after watching her do the lead change a few more times. "But you're doing it... weird. Here," he said, spurring Satchmo into motion. "You go over there and watch." When Stevie and Jack Rabbit were by the gate, he went on. "It looks like you're doing the lead change with his shoulders. That's what it looks like now, anyway. Earlier, you did a flying lead change almost perfect. Now, though... I don't know what you're doing."

Stevie started to tell him how she was doing it, but he wasn't finished yet.

"You need to direct the lead with his hindquarters," Blake said. "Not his shoulders. The foundation of a flying lead change is in the hindquarters."

Stevie had heard all of this before. She tried to shift her awareness of Jack Rabbit to include his hindquarters. It felt... odd. To Jack Rabbit as well, who shifted and stamped.

"Are you listening, Stevie?" Blake asked.

She brought her attention back to Blake. "Yes. I'm listening."

"Uh huh," Blake said. "Maybe we should do the lead change exercises on Rain—"

"No," Stevie said, and Jack Rabbit snorted agreement.

"Fine," Blake said, heading her off. "But I don't want you picking up any bad habits. If you're going to compete in the arena you have to learn proper lead changes."

"But if we're doing it—"

"I said *proper* lead changes," Blake interrupted her. "Look, this is how Mom taught me to do it. I still remember seeing her ride. Seeing you ride earlier, it was like watching her again, at least up until that idiotic finale. The key is in positioning the hindquarters with your legs..."

Stevie watched Blake's lips move but she no longer listened to his words. *Just like your mother.* Dad's words came back to her, with Blake's voice.

She let Blake continue to talk, uninterrupted. She didn't tell him that she didn't want to train with Rain. And that she didn't want to learn to ride—or do anything else—like Mom. She almost wished she could take back that glorious ride around the pasture. She nodded when Blake seemed to expect it. And she stroked Jack Rabbit's neck. She and Jack Rabbit would do it their own way.

Chapter 7
Stevie's First Race

AFTER THREE WEEKS of breakfast alone with Blake, Dad still sleeping heavily in his room despite the dawn, Stevie had become used to Dad's morning absence. She hadn't thought about Dad's new habit for the last week.

She thought of it today, though, as she chewed her buttered toast, barely tasting it, not remembering that she had forgotten to layer it with jelly until she had eaten half of it. She couldn't believe Dad would miss her first race. It didn't seem possible.

She couldn't believe she had forgotten the jelly either. She had been telling herself all morning she wasn't nervous. *I'm not nervous.* Over and over, like a mantra. The toast made a liar of her.

She looked at the half of toast still in her hand, thought about putting jelly on it, to silence her sudden flair of nerves. She decided not to bother. It didn't matter. Jelly or no jelly wasn't important. Then she did it anyway—a racing girl needed all the energy she could get—pulling the jelly jar across the table from where Blake had been hoarding it.

"Gross," Blake said, watching her spread jelly over the half-eaten toast with the spoon from the jar. "That's like double dipping."

Stevie finished and gave Blake a look. "That just means I get to lick the spoon," she said, and popped it into her mouth.

Blake had tried to tell her, indirectly, that Dad would miss her first race. She had nodded when Blake spoke, but she hadn't believed it. There was no way Dad would miss her race. She had even talked to Dad about it the night before.

"Maybe," he had said, and that had been the end of it. She had believed that *maybe* meant *yes*. Because she wanted to believe it.

Just before breakfast, fresh out of her shower, wearing the new clothes she and Michelle had picked out for her first race of the summer, she had stood in front of Dad's door, new hat held in her left hand, right hand raised, wanting to knock. Through the door she could hear Dad breathing his slow, heavy breaths, sometimes almost snoring.

She gave a quick, low knock, three light raps. She heard his breathing pause, then resume.

She didn't knock again. Maybe he would make it to the race later, even if he didn't come with her and Blake and Jack Rabbit.

Stevie put the thoroughly licked spoon down on her plate and picked up her toast again. But she just looked at it.

"Nervous?" Blake asked.

"No," Stevie said, then, "Yes."

"Why?" Blake asked, his face becoming a shade more innocent. "I thought this was the race you would be OK not winning." He pitched his voice higher, his imitation of Stevie. "'Third or fourth place is fine', you said. 'Maybe I won't even place at all. This is just my first race, you know.'"

Stevie stuck her tongue out at him, then took a big bite of her toast and jelly so she wouldn't have to respond further.

After they had finished eating and put everything away in the kitchen, Stevie found herself standing outside Dad's door once again, listening to him. She raised her hand to knock, but stopped before she did. She sighed and leaned her head against the molding of the doorframe.

She wanted Dad to be there. She felt that without Dad she would be there all alone. Blake would be there, of course, but so would Shannon. Blake was a divided audience these days. And Blake was also her coach, constantly trying to change how she and Jack Rabbit worked together. She wanted Dad to see her ride. To see her at all. To be there.

She wished Edwin would be there too. She had been missing him more this past week as she practiced and worked around the farm. Just like Thanksgiving, she kept expecting to see him, kept wanting to tell him about the upcoming race. Kept remembering that he was gone.

Blake's hand on her shoulder made Stevie stand up straight again. "Bring home a ribbon," Blake said, looking away as Stevie ran a knuckle under each eye, pushing away the small tears that had begun to form. "That'll teach him to miss a race."

Stevie nodded. "Yeah," she said. She managed a tight smile, for Blake's sake. "That'll teach him."

Jack Rabbit waited for her in his stall, where she had put him last night after grooming him and checking his hooves and shoes for the hundredth time. In the cool morning light his red coat muted to a rich brown and gleamed like he was glossed. The sight of him took Stevie's breath away. Jack Rabbit caught her eye and raised his head, preening.

"You're ready to race, aren't you boy?" she asked.

Jack Rabbit nodded, then danced a couple steps, conveying the urge to burst out of the stall and run like the wind.

Stevie laughed.

She took the time to groom him once more with the curry brush, then cleaned out his hooves and put on his travel boots. When she was ready, Jack Rabbit lowered his head for her to put on the halter and lead. He wasn't nervous at all. He *wanted* to race. She could feel it in his muscles, see it in his eyes—and in her mind.

For the past week, she and Blake had held Jack Rabbit to a slow pace in her practices. He had tugged against the reins and almost revolted until Stevie made it clear that she would let him charge as fast he could in the race on Saturday. He had still been antsy, but allowed her to hold him back. Today, though, was the day they had both been waiting for. There would be no holding back. Stevie gave him a tight hug around the neck, then led him out of the stall.

Jack Rabbit pulled back on the lead rope when Stevie turned toward the corral doors. He gestured toward the main doors with his head. The truck is *that* way.

Still no words, but the images came into Stevie's mind, of her leading Jack Rabbit out the big front doors into the morning sunlight, to the ramp of the trailer. Then Jack Rabbit stepping into the trailer, head held high, a horse on his way to take on all comers and *win*.

Stevie hesitated. Jack Rabbit had never been the easiest horse to get into a trailer, sometimes taking ten to fifteen minutes to calm down, respond to direction, and finally walk up the ramp.

Jack Rabbit snorted. The meaning Stevie felt from the big horse was that those times he hadn't been going to race. He pulled on the lead rope again, toward the main doors.

Stevie bit her lip. Then smiled. "OK, boy. Let's go race."

Blake looked at them in surprise when Stevie led Jack Rabbit out the main doors of the barn. He stood by the gate to the corral. "Aren't you going to work him out first?"

Stevie shook her head. "Nope." She led Jack Rabbit, both of them holding their heads high, until they stood at the foot of the ramp.

"Everything ready?" Stevie asked Blake.

"Ready when you are," Blake said.

Stevie led Jack Rabbit up the ramp into the trailer. Jack Rabbit started to pull back when the trailer shifted under their weight, but recovered quickly, then followed her into the darkness. He remained still while she put the chest bar in place and tied his lead rope in a panic knot. Once he was secured, Stevie stroked his nose and he nickered and nudged her. He was ready, she should get moving already. Stevie smiled and slipped out the escape door. She came back to the rear of the trailer and helped Blake raise the ramp and secure it.

"Good job," Blake said. "That was a lot less fuss than the last time I tried to trailer him."

"He likes me better."

"Looks like someone came to see you off."

Stevie perked up and turned to face the front of the house. Her smile faltered when she saw that Dad wasn't standing there. No one was.

"I meant over there," Blake said, pointing.

Stevie followed the line of his arm and saw Rain standing by the pasture gate on the far side of the corral.

"Oh."

Good luck. Rain's voice, as clear in Stevie's mind as if they stood face to face, instead of separated by almost a hundred feet.

Stevie turned her back on Rain and went to climb into the pickup.

The parking lot and loading zones of the Todd-Whatley-Lige Hammock Memorial Arena in Hugo were already crowded by the time they arrived. Stevie helped get Jack Rabbit out of the trailer, then left him with Blake when Shannon arrived.

Michelle Hunter found Stevie standing in the line to get her official number. Michelle emerged out of the crowd around Stevie with a smile and a sneaky look that Stevie didn't quite trust.

Michelle's eyes twinkled as they did whenever she had something to say that she wasn't saying yet. Stevie resisted the urge to ask what it was. That would just make Michelle take even longer to get around to it. Whatever it was.

Michelle laughed, as if she had heard Stevie's thoughts. Then she made a spinning gesture with her right hand. "Spin around, spin around," she said. "Let's see how you look."

Stevie adjusted her hat to a jaunty angle, hooked her thumbs in her belt loops, and spun around on the heels of her new roper boots.

"Excellent," Michelle said. "We'll make a proper country girl out of you again in no time."

"I couldn't be more country," Stevie said, poking Michelle in the shoulder with her finger. "You were the one who kept wanting to go shopping in the city."

"Guess who I saw as I was trying to find you," Michelle said, smiling. "Guess."

Stevie sighed and shook her head. She didn't have to guess. "Travis Delozier?" she said, getting it over with. Michelle hadn't been capable of talking about anyone else for the past three weeks, though Travis hadn't been to the ranch since that awful Sunday afternoon. Stevie had seen him once or twice around Antlers, but hadn't spoken to him. Michelle, though, seemed to run into him everywhere. And insisted on telling Stevie about it every time.

Michelle looked scandalized. "So you knew he was here? Did you two come together?"

"No," Stevie said. "We didn't come together. And I didn't know he was here."

"Really," Michelle said. She looked unconvinced. "He knew *you* were here. In fact," she went on, leaning closer to Stevie, "he told me where to find you."

Stevie sighed again, wondering why she even bothered. She looked up at the white banner stretched over her head, the one that said in large black letters, "Barrel Racers Registration." "I can't imagine how he knew."

The line moved, and Stevie and Michelle moved with it, getting closer to the front.

"Maybe he's stalking you," Michelle said.

Stevie snorted, sounding like Jack Rabbit to herself, and looked back at Michelle. "He's probably worried that you're stalking *him*."

Michelle looked shocked, but her eyes twinkled.

"Following him around," Stevie went on before Michelle could say anything. "Reporting on his every move. The poor guy is probably scared stiff, wondering when you'll show up and terrorize his family and threaten his pet bunny—"

"He has a pet bunny?"

"I don't know," Stevie said. "OK, yes. But that was years ago. And that's not the point. If he *does* still have a pet rabbit, he's probably frightened of what you'll do to it when he finally tells you that he's not—"

"Are you here to race?" asked the man behind the table. "Or to spoil the plot of *Fatal Attraction*?"

"Sorry," Stevie said. "My name is Buckbee. Stevie Buckbee." She gave her information to the man, and then handed over the entry fee, and took the printed number he gave her.

She and Michelle walked away from the table, then stopped so Michelle could help her pin the number to the back of her shirt.

"I think it's so cute," Michelle said.

"What?" Stevie asked, trying to look over her shoulder at Michelle.

"You can call your first child 'Bunny'."

Stevie noticed other people around them now, standing and watching. Listening and smiling. Stevie felt her face and ears get warm. "Oh, shut up."

"That wouldn't be her name, of course," Michelle continued, ignoring her, talking just a bit louder now, for their audience. "Though it could be. But I was thinking more of a special nickname."

"Did you say your name was Buckbee?" A woman's voice penetrated Stevie's mortification. Stevie gave Michelle, who looked as innocent as could be, one last glare, then swiveled her neck to face the plump, older woman now standing in front of her.

The woman stood only an inch or two taller than Stevie, with her long, wispy salt-and-pepper hair pulled back from her face. Her skin was dark from a combination of outdoor sun and Native American color. The woman smiled at Stevie when their eyes met, emphasizing the wrinkles around her eyes, and Stevie wondered just how much of Michelle's little fantasy the woman had overheard. She tried to keep her face from growing redder, and failed. She looked down, blocking the woman's face with the brim of her hat. Her ears seemed to radiate heat.

Stevie made herself look up and meet the woman's gaze again. She tried to remember the woman's question. "I'm sorry," she said after a second. "What did you ask?"

"I don't mean to intrude," the woman said, still smiling, and obviously more than willing to intrude. "But did I overhear you saying your name is Buckbee?"

"Yes, ma'am. My name's Stevie Buckbee."

"Well, now, bless your heart. Are you Jake and Stephanie's daughter?"

Jake and Stephanie. Stevie's jaw clenched and her teeth ground together, and her ears became warm again for an entirely different reason. "Yes," she said, her voice tight. Her earliest memories included that phrase—Jake and Stephanie—but never in a good way. At family gatherings, whispered, but not low enough to keep Stevie from hearing. *Did you hear Jake and Stephanie are having problems?*

If the woman noticed Stevie's discomfort, she didn't show it. Her smile remained as bright as before. "I knew it," she said. "You're the spitting image of Stephanie Blake."

Stevie wanted to say that she didn't look *anything* like her mother. But the woman didn't even pause to take a breath.

"I knew it when I saw you, and then when I heard you talking I knew you just had to be Stephanie's little girl, all grown up and riding, just like her. She used to ride here every year, from the time she was your age..."

The woman kept talking, but Stevie didn't hear her. She could only hear the voices in her head. Aunt Mary's voice. *No, Jake and Stephanie aren't here. Just Jake and the kids. Did you hear? She left him. Up and gone away. No word in weeks—*

The woman had taken Stevie's left hand and was pulling her along. "If you have a few minutes," the woman was saying, as unconcerned about Stevie's schedule as she was about intruding, "there's someone you have to meet."

Stevie wanted to protest, but couldn't push any words out of her throat. She wanted to pull back, but the woman's grip was like a leathery claw, trapping her and marching her forward like an errant little girl on her way to the principal's office. Stevie looked over her shoulder to make sure that Michelle was following. She was. Michelle caught her eye and gave her a wane smile and a shrug.

"I just know you're going to want to meet Rita," the woman was saying as they weaved around men and women and children in denim and cowboy cut shirts and boots and wide-brimmed hats. "I saw her just a few minutes before I saw you. Isn't that something? Seeing both of you like that? After all these years?" The woman didn't seem to need answers. She led Stevie and Michelle into the arena, around the base of a set of wooden bleachers, and paused. "Now, I know I saw Rita around here..."

Stevie made another try to retrieve her hand. "That's OK," she said. "I really need to get back—"

The woman didn't let go. She glanced at Stevie, then turned her gaze back to the bleachers, still searching. "Don't be silly, dear. The race doesn't start for an hour yet." She paused again. "There she is." She waved with her free hand. "Rita!" she called. "Rita Kaltenbach!"

Stevie saw a woman seated in the bleachers look up. The woman holding Stevie prisoner waved more vigorously, and the woman in the stands stood and walked down to them.

Rita Kaltenbach was at least as old as Stevie's captor, though leaner, with even more wrinkles around her eyes, a tan that came entirely from the sun, and her long hair completely white. She wore neat but well-worn jeans and a cowboy shirt. She looked tall coming down the bleachers, but when she came off the last step her pale blue eyes were level with Stevie's.

Those eyes looked at Stevie and she felt an urge to look away. Stevie blinked instead. Rita Kaltenbach didn't look familiar, but something about the name caught her attention. A hint of a smile played around Rita Kaltenbach's thin lips.

"Stevie Buckbee," the woman holding Stevie's hand said, "I want you to meet Rita Kaltenbach. Rita, you remember Stephanie Blake, of course. This is her daughter, Stevie."

Rita Kaltenbach's face showed mild surprise. She reached out her right hand. "Call me Rita."

Stevie hesitated, not wanting to lose both her hands, but then she held out her right hand, and they shook. "Nice to meet you, Rita."

Rita gave a laugh. "You don't look like it's all that nice." She faced the other woman. "You can let go of her hand now, Lavena."

Stevie's hand finally came free, and Lavena smiled sheepishly. Then she recovered. "Stevie," she said, "Ms. Kaltenbach—I mean, Rita—taught your mother how to ride."

Rita laughed again. "I tried, anyway. Girls like Stephanie Blake are hard to teach anything."

Stevie remembered Rita Kaltenbach then. Not the woman herself. But the name. Rita Kaltenbach had taught Mom, and it was she who had first trained Rain, Mom's horse. And Stevie remembered that Blake had been taking riding lessons from her, as well. Even after Mom left, Blake had gone to her for lessons. But that had ended years ago. Stevie recalled that Rita Kaltenbach had moved away.

"Doesn't she look just like Stephanie, though?" Lavena was saying. "All dressed up and ready to race?"

Stevie started to protest—again—that she didn't look anything like her mother, but Rita's eyes locked onto Stevie's. Stevie felt exposed, and she kept her mouth closed. She felt the warmth returning to her face.

"Not really, no," Rita said. "She's got more of her father in her."

Stevie's opinion of Rita Kaltenbach rose, and she almost smiled.

"But you can see Stephanie in there too," Rita added, heading off a protest from Lavena. Rita looked Stevie up and down, and Stevie's smiled ended before it began. She felt like a horse being examined as part of a trade. "I'll bet she rides like Stephanie, though. I can see that in her."

Stevie finally found her voice. "I—I ride like me," she said. She stood up straighter as she said it, defying Ms. Rita Kaltenbach to contradict her.

But Rita just smiled. "I'll bet you do." The woman looked Stevie up and down again, then looked into her eyes one more time. "I'll bet you do, at that. Your Mom was hard to teach, as well. Your Mom was an excellent rider, though. There are worse people you could ride like. Who's teaching you?"

Stevie wanted to protest that she wasn't hard to teach. And wanted to say—but no seemed to be interested—that she didn't ride like her mother. So she said only, "Blake. My brother."

Rita nodded. "Blake's a good boy, a natural rider."

Stevie opened her mouth to agree with Rita. Stevie almost told her how Blake had decided to become an engineer, or an architect, instead of riding. Almost shared her shock. But she stopped herself, because she had only just met Rita. And Rita had been Mom's riding teacher. And because Rita hadn't stopped talking.

"I guess I'll see how good a teacher he is today, won't I?"

Michelle laughed behind Stevie. "No pressure there," she said.

Rita's eyes moved to look at Michelle. Lavena looked surprised, confused maybe, as if this was the first time she had seen the girl Stevie was talking to when Lavena grabbed her and pulled her away to "meet someone."

Stevie introduced Michelle to Rita. And then Lavena. After that there was an awkward pause. Stevie was unsure how to proceed—or how to leave without seeming rude. Not that either of the women seemed to care that *they* had been rude—

"You probably need to get back to your horse," Rita said, saving Stevie the burden of trying to figure out what to say to two strange women. "I look forward to seeing you ride."

Trying not to say good-bye too quickly, or to appear like she was running away, Stevie took Michelle's hand and gripped tightly as she did both.

The crowd opened and closed around them again, but now Stevie avoided looking anyone in the eyes. She still held Michelle's hand. She didn't want to let go. She adjusted her hat with her free hand, blocking her face. So that no one else could recognize her. Or tell her how much she looked like Mom. Or tell her how she should ride.

Michelle gave her hand a squeeze, reassuring Stevie. "You'll do great."

Stevie nodded. She would show them.

"You ready?" Blake asked.

Above him, in the saddle, Stevie nodded. She hoped she didn't look as sick as she felt. Sick or not, though, she was ready.

She clenched the reins and looked out at the bright arena, at the floor covered with dirt churned up by hundreds of hooves, at the three barrels arranged and waiting for her, and listened to the sounds of the crowd and the blare of the announcer. Stevie's stomach had climbed up into her chest and she wanted to throw up. The last time she had felt this nervous had been the first day of school in Tulsa, walking alone and friendless into the huge box-like building with its reflective windows and more students and teachers than even lived in her hometown. She had managed to not throw up that day. She wouldn't throw up now.

She could feel Jack Rabbit's excitement. The horse trembled, held back by her grip on the reins and her legs around his ribs. He was ready too.

Jack Rabbit wanted to *race.*

And, nervous or not, so did she.

"Barrel racing is won in the turns," Blake said.

Stevie only nodded. She knew that. Because how many times had he said that in the last ten minutes? In the last three weeks? She wasn't sure she could count that high.

In practice he always followed up that advice with, "And to win the turns you have to control the lead changes." Because they had been arguing about how she did her lead changes every day for the last three weeks. He insisted she was doing it wrong, and she insisted that it was *her* way, hers and Jack Rabbit's. Once, at dinner, Blake had tried to appeal to Dad. But Dad had only looked at Stevie, then at Blake. "Work it out," he had said, then went back to eating.

Today, though, Blake said nothing else. He looked up and caught Stevie's eye and she managed a tight smile for him.

"Remember," Blake said. "You don't have to win this one."

Her smile faded. "Yes, I do." She hadn't told him about Rita Kaltenbach. Stevie was riding for herself, for Jack Rabbit, and for Blake now. *No pressure there.* All she felt was pressure, from everywhere.

"Go get 'em," Blake said, and he left her there to wait for the flag.

Jack Rabbit tensed and wanted to fidget.

"Calm down, boy," she said. "Almost..."

The flag whipped down.

"Hyah!" Stevie yelled, and Jack Rabbit uncoiled like a steel spring.

They surged forward, horse and girl, angling toward the first barrel, aiming at the point halfway between the first and third barrels—just like Blake had taught her.

"You can't just ride straight to the first barrel," Blake had told her over and over, and she could almost hear him tell her again now over the sound of the crowd and the drumbeat of Jack Rabbit's hooves. "It's harder on the horse and you're more likely to tip the barrel."

Just past halfway to the first barrel, Stevie tightened their angle of approach and pulled back on Jack Rabbit to keep him from taking the first barrel too fast. She aimed for a pocket of four feet or less, and nailed it.

As she and Jack Rabbit leaned into the turn, she reached with her mind, felt his forelegs as her own, and directed his first lead change. Jack Rabbit no longer resisted when she did that, but the result wasn't as smooth at full speed as it had been in practice. She felt the stutter in his muscles, the shock of hard impact in his bones, felt them in her own muscles and bones.

But they cleared the barrel by at least a foot and began accelerating into the second leg of the race even before they had finished the turn.

She kept her torso low as Jack Rabbit stretched into the ninety feet between the first and second barrels. The distance disappeared almost before she could slow him down again, and they were into the second turn.

She hit the pocket closer this time, coming within three feet of the barrel. She bared her teeth in satisfaction—pocketing that close, just like a professional—and then grimaced from pain as the stress on Jack Rabbit's muscles and joints slammed into her, especially her left wrist. She kept both Jack Rabbit and herself together, though, navigating the turn and heading toward the last barrel.

Her left wrist throbbed now with every beat of Jack Rabbit's left foreleg. But still they raced forward, and the sixty feet to the third barrel were gone in a blur of dirt and spectators' faces. The sound of the crowd changed, she noticed, but she had no time to pay attention as they went into the final turn.

No fancy pocketing this time. It was all Stevie could do to concentrate on not hitting the barrel as they took the turn. Jack Rabbit almost stumbled, his weight and momentum almost overpowering muscle and bone, but Stevie reached even deeper and didn't let him falter. The pain in her left wrist, like a hammer slamming down on it, made her cry out and put tears in her eyes. But she didn't let go of the reins. And Jack Rabbit came around fast.

Coming out of the turn, she let Jack Rabbit have his head. Because she had planned to, and because she couldn't stop him now if she wanted to. He pulled them forward, toward the gate, an earthquake in motion, a shockwave, a force of nature let loose in the arena. Stevie forgot the pain in her wrist and laughed with the joy of the run, tears still in her eyes, as they went through the gate, wondering if they had gone too fast for the people in the stands to even see them.

Once through the gate, as she tried to pull up, the pain came back, shooting up her arm. She bit back the cry this time, but her left hand couldn't maintain its grip on the reins. She managed to rein Jack Rabbit in with just her right hand, her left held to her chest.

Jack Rabbit came to a lopsided stop, pulling right. His excitement was still high and he pranced. Stevie wanted to pat him to calm him down, but with only one hand it was all she could to do keep him reined in, and turn him to face the gate again.

Then Blake was there, grabbing Jack Rabbit's bridle and yelling, "What the hell were you—?"

The rest of his outrage was drowned by the roar of the crowd. Stevie glanced up to see the scoreboard just as the announcer said, "And that's newcomer Stevie Buckbee with an amazing 16.68 run—"

16.68

The numbers blazed on the scoreboard and burned into the back of Stevie's eyes and rang in her ears. Blake was still yelling at her, and the announcer continued saying something over the crowd noise, but Stevie heard none of it.

She had come in under seventeen seconds. On her first race.

She had beat the best time of the morning, an impressive 17:10 set by Lynn Gascon, by nearly half a second.

"I won," Stevie said, shocked. And she had been thinking third or fourth place would have been great. Her first race, and she had won.

"You haven't won yet," Blake said. His voice still had an angry edge, but Stevie could see that even Blake had been impressed by her time.

Jack Rabbit didn't understand seconds or hundredths of a second, but he understood winning. If Blake hadn't been holding his bridle, Jack Rabbit would've reared.

"I should withdraw your name from the event," Blake said, leading the still-excited Jack Rabbit while Stevie walked beside him. "I should pack up you and Jack Rabbit and go home."

Stevie had brought her right leg over and slid out of the saddle, acting jaunty to hide the pain in her wrist—and the fact that she couldn't use it to get down. The jolt of landing, though, had been painful, and she clutched her wrist with her right hand, trying not to feel like she was holding it together. She didn't know what had happened, what she must've done, to sprain her wrist. Had she been pulling too hard on the reins? Another answer occurred to her, but she didn't want to think about it.

"What?" Stevie said, as Blake's words finally penetrated the joy of winning and the fog of pain. "Don't you dare! I *won*."

"You haven't won yet," Blake said again, his voice beginning to rise. "And I'm not even sure how you finished the race at all. What the hell—" He paused, and lowered his voice again. "What did you think you were doing? Taking the turns that way?"

"We did it our way," Stevie said. "Mine and Jack Rabbit's."

"You did it *wrong*."

Stevie hadn't expected Blake's anger. She pressed her wrist to her chest. "Why aren't you happy that I won?"

"You haven't—" Blake started, then paused, getting himself under control again. "Skip that. Fine. You won. Yippee for you. But winning doesn't excuse almost laming a good horse."

Stevie noticed people they passed were looking at them. Some of them were listening.

"What are you talking about?" she asked, keeping her voice low. "Look at him," she added, letting go of her wrist just long enough to point at Jack Rabbit. "He's great. He's practically *dancing*."

Blake looked at Stevie, his eyes cold. "Sure, he looks fine now." He didn't lower his voice any more than before. "No thanks to *you*, by the way. But I'll have to have Dr. Siemers come out and make sure you didn't lame him."

"I didn't lame Jack Rabbit," Stevie said. "Stop talking like that."

"We won't know for sure until Dr. Siemers can check him out."

"That's one helluva horse you got there," a man's voice said. Stevie turned to see a tall, thin man walking up to them. He nodded to Blake and Stevie, and pushed his hat back on his head. "If you don't mind me saying. Saw you ride, Miss. Don't often see a horse that can take those kind of turns. He'd be a fine cutting horse."

Jack Rabbit perked his ears at the praise, and Stevie beamed. "Thanks."

Blake said nothing.

The man gave them another nod and went on his way.

"Stevie!" Michelle came running up behind them. "That was amazing."

Stevie smiled. "Thanks."

"I thought you were going to spill on the second turn," Michelle went on. "And then again on the third turn. But you held on, and here you are, just waiting for your trophy." She gave Stevie a big smile.

Stevie's own smile went slack at the word *spill*. There had never been any chance of her spilling. Didn't anyone believe she deserved to win?

Mounting Jack Rabbit again for the final ceremony proved difficult. The pain in her left wrist made it impossible to grip anything with that hand, and putting any kind of weight on it was out of the question. She finally managed it by holding the reins in her teeth and pulling herself up with just her right hand.

"What's wrong with your wrist?" Blake asked.

She felt precarious in the saddle, panting from the pain and exertion, with her left wrist useless. But Jack Rabbit had calmed down and was eager to parade in front of the other horses, so he cooperated. She could do this.

"I sprained it, I guess," she said.

Blake looked unwilling to accept that, but didn't question her further.

Accepting the trophy from the judges created another challenge. For most of the ceremony, she held her wrist—casually, she hoped—against her hip. She had to tuck the trophy awkwardly under her left arm, though, reins loose while she used her feet and legs to direct Jack Rabbit and shake hands with the judges and other riders.

Lynn Gascon, who had come in second in their division, congratulated her, then said, "That's a great horse you have there."

Despite the pain and the awkwardness, Stevie's grin hadn't faded since coming into the arena again, announced as the winner. "I know," she said. She started to say more, extolling Jack Rabbit's spirit and determination, but Lynn gave her a *Do you?* look, and turned away, leaving Stevie with her mouth hanging open.

She saw Travis Delozier in the stands then. He was with his parents. He smiled at her and waved, and Stevie felt her grin return. She waved back. Travis's mother met Stevie's eyes, but looked away before Stevie could wave to her.

Stevie rode out of the arena, looking for Blake, and saw him talking with Rita Kaltenbach. Stevie wondered where Shannon had gone.

Rita nodded when she saw Stevie and Jack Rabbit walking toward them. Stevie couldn't read Rita's expression, but she saw Rita's eyes drop to her wrist—not the trophy still clutched against Stevie's chest with her left arm; but at Stevie's *wrist*—and then come back to Stevie's eyes. As if Rita knew about the pain. And knew more about it than Stevie did.

Rita said good-bye to Blake and walked away before Stevie reached them. Stevie watched Rita go, wondering how her ride had reflected on Blake's teaching. Then she squeezed the trophy tighter. She had won her first race. She couldn't have done any better. So why wasn't everyone happy for her?

"Are you ready to go?" Blake asked, looking up at Stevie.

Stevie sighed, then nodded. At least Jack Rabbit was happy. And the big horse remained in a good mood even as they walked him into the trailer to head home.

Chapter 8
Stupid Men

"GOOD JOB," DAD said when Stevie posed in the door of his office, trophy held up in her right hand. He even smiled, and stood up to give Stevie a congratulatory hug. Stevie hugged him as tight as she could without hurting her wrist too much. *Good job* and a hug from Dad almost made up for him not being there.

Then she put the trophy on his desk and ran back outside to help Blake get Jack Rabbit out of the trailer.

She had trouble grooming Jack Rabbit with just one hand. It wasn't impossible. Just awkward. Even more so because Jack Rabbit wouldn't stand still. He wanted to get to the pasture, to the other horses. Like her, Jack Rabbit wanted an audience to tell his story of winning.

After Stevie finished grooming Jack Rabbit, Blake insisted on examining all of his legs and hooves before she could lead him to the pasture.

"There's nothing wrong with his legs," Stevie said, pressing her wrist to her chest again. Pressure helped, and warmth.

Blake didn't answer. He had been silent all the way home. He just looked at her, then continued his examination, running his fingers over the muscles and joints, looking for swelling or signs of sensitivity.

115

Stevie's only consolation was that Jack Rabbit didn't hold still for Blake any better than he had for Stevie.

Finally, Blake grunted and stood up straight. "I didn't find anything, but that doesn't mean he's not hurt—"

"He's not hurt," Stevie said. "There's nothing wrong with him."

Blake met her eyes. "You don't know that."

Before Stevie could protest that she did *too* know that—Jack Rabbit's health and strength were plainly visible to her—Blake turned and walked away.

She led Jack Rabbit to the pasture and took off his halter. She stood and watched him trot to rejoin the other horses, who perked up to watch him. Satchmo seemed unimpressed, not looking up, only flicking an ear as if to shoo away a fly. But Buckaroo and the other geldings crowded around as Jack Rabbit pranced and ducked and raised his head and swished his tail, telling the story of the race.

The images Stevie picked up showed the race from Jack Rabbit's perspective, the barrels and the tight turns rushing at her at eye level, culminating in the headlong rush from the last barrel to the gate. The sensations of speed and power washed over Stevie and she relived the race with her horse. She almost forgot to be upset at Blake.

The other horses nickered and stamped their approval—except Satchmo. The blue roan no longer stood apart. He had joined the cluster of horses, on the fringe. He still displayed no outward signs of interest, but Stevie could tell that even he was impressed.

You would think he ran the race alone. Rain's voice in her head pulled Stevie's attention. The old mare stood to the side, away from the group around Jack Rabbit, her blanket of spots catching the late afternoon sunshine and making her look ten years younger. *Congratulations, Stevie.*

Stevie smiled. She still hadn't forgiven Rain. But she had won her first barrel race. She could be nice to anyone. Even Rain.

You met Rita.

Not a question. Stevie realized she had been thinking of the look on Rita Kaltenbach's face as the old woman had talked to Blake. Neither Rita nor Blake had congratulated her.

A different image of Rita appeared in Stevie's mind. Younger, still middle-aged but with fewer wrinkles around her eyes and some sun-bleached color in her hair. The look on this Rita's face was pleased approval. Not at all like the look Stevie had seen earlier.

Neither of them know what you did.

Stevie felt the pain in her wrist again. She looked at Rain. The horse met her eyes. *For Jack Rabbit.*

Stevie's right hand found her left wrist again and squeezed it, soothing the ache—some. "We ran the race together," she said. "Jack Rabbit and me."

Not the way he tells it.

Stevie turned her back on Rain and left the pasture.

There was no smile and no look of approval on Dad's face at dinner. While Stevie had been showering, then re-arranging the contents of her shelves to find just the right spot to better display her new trophy, Blake must have been talking to Dad.

Dad didn't even wait for her to sit down. "Do you know how much it costs just to have Vincent Siemers visit?"

Stevie rested her left hand in her lap as she sat down. "Then don't have him come," she said. "There's nothing wrong with Jack Rabbit."

Dad looked at her. "And I'm supposed to trust *your* judgment on this?"

"Yes!" Stevie said. Dad's face clouded, but Stevie rushed on before he could speak. "I know as much about horses as Blake does—" Blake grunted. Stevie ignored him. "—and he knows it. I didn't do anything wrong."

"Nothing wrong?" Blake said. "If you could've seen how you took those turns—"

"I took them the way you taught me," Stevie said, glaring at her brother across the table.

"I'm not sure I've managed to teach you *anything*." Before Stevie could protest again, he said, "No! Do you know what Rita Kaltenbach told me after your race? Do you?" Stevie started to refuse to answer, but he didn't wait. "She told me that I should have someone else teach you. Because *obviously* I wasn't up to it. Maybe it wasn't my fault, she said. Maybe you're just too damn *stubborn*."

Stevie leaned forward and pointed a stiff finger at Blake. "I am *not* stubborn! But maybe that wouldn't be a bad idea. Maybe I do need a new teacher. One that won't be mad when I win a race."

"You only won because Jack Rabbit carried you."

Stevie opened her mouth to protest. But she didn't know what to say to that. She agreed with him—because she and Jack Rabbit were a team—but not with the way he said it.

"And maybe I'm tired of trying to teach you," Blake went on, overriding her. "Maybe I could finally have some free time."

"To spend with Shannon?" Stevie asked. It sounded stupid and petty as soon as she said it, but it was the only thing that came to mind. And, somehow, Shannon was probably to blame.

"To spend away from *you*," Blake said.

Stevie's jaw dropped in shock. "Well, maybe I don't want you to teach me anymore." She wished she hadn't said that. Because she did want him to keep teaching her. She needed him too. But he was making her so *mad*. Why couldn't he just congratulate her? She had won. What else did he want from her? Stevie's eyes locked on his and she glared at him while he glared back. She saw he was about to say something, and she opened her own mouth to rebut him.

"Hold on," Dad said. Both of them stopped with their mouths open. But they didn't look away. They continued to glare at each other. "Do you know how much paying a trainer would cost?"

Surprised, Stevie looked at Dad. She wasn't sure what she had expected him to say. *Work it out*, maybe. Or, *You two shut up and eat.* But not, *Do you know how much paying a trainer would cost?* He wasn't seriously considering letting Blake stop teaching her, was he? Or maybe—

"You could teach me," Stevie said, the words rushing out before she could try not to hope that maybe Dad would come back to her.

Dad didn't meet her eyes, and her hope withered before it could bloom. "After what Blake tells me about your race—"

Her dying hope sparked into anger. "Blake wouldn't have to tell you about my race," she said, her voice rising, "if you had *been there.*"

Anger showed in Dad's eyes, and Stevie saw the muscles in his cheek bunch. He swallowed and his lips started to curl back. Stevie braced herself for the verbal onslaught. She wouldn't take back what she had said. She wouldn't feel guilty. Because she was *right.* Dad should have been there, watching her. He should have been there from the beginning, helping her ride. He should have been there, in Tulsa, to pick her up that first day. He should never have sent her to Tulsa in the first place.

But then the anger in Dad's eyes faded, the muscles of his jaw unclenched, and he looked down at his plate. He picked up his fork, stabbed it into his dinner, and proceeded to eat.

Stevie didn't know what to say. Her anger flared, and she opened her mouth. She wanted to tell Dad what she was thinking. That he *should* have been there. He *should* have seen her race and win. It wasn't fair that he had stayed home. He hadn't been fair to her. She wanted to say all of that, and more, but Dad didn't look at her. He kept his eyes on his plate as he ate. And her anger collapsed into guilt.

She looked at Blake. He met her gaze, but his face was passive. She couldn't tell what he was thinking. Then Blake looked down and began to eat, as well.

Stevie looked at her own plate, but she didn't see the food. She wanted to tell Dad she was sorry. But she didn't. Because he hadn't said it to her.

Dr. Vincent Siemers, D.V.M., came to the ranch first thing Monday morning. Dad got up and met him, the earliest Stevie had seen Dad rise since she had come home from Tulsa. He even had breakfast with her and Blake. Both Dad and Blake ignored her surprised looks, pretending, she decided, that this was normal. She wasn't sure she would ever understand men.

Stevie watched the vet examine Jack Rabbit, and nodded in agreement when Dr. Siemers pronounced Jack Rabbit "as healthy as a horse." Dad didn't look convinced, but he accepted the doctor's word. Because, Stevie knew, insisting on a more thorough examination meant taking Jack Rabbit somewhere he could be x-rayed. Dr. Siemers saw no reason for that to happen, but he did say he'd come back in a week to check on Jack Rabbit again—just to be sure.

Stevie's own prognosis, unfortunately, wasn't as good. She made it almost to lunch before the effort of ignoring the pain in her left wrist became too much. She had coddled the wrist all day Sunday, even wrapped it with a spare Ace bandage, but the pain had not subsided. And when she tried to use it Monday, having wrapped the bandages as tight as she could, the grind of bones on nerves and tendons brought tears to her eyes. Blake drove her into town.

She and Blake hadn't talked since dinner Saturday night. He hadn't been around—off with Shannon, Stevie was sure—but even if he had been home, Stevie would've refused to talk to him. Monday, he had only talked to her to tell her what to do. And then, when he saw the swelling in her wrist and the tears in her eyes, he had insisted that he take her to see the doctor.

The family doctor, Dr. Weaver, x-rayed Stevie's wrist, then pointed to several minor stress fractures at the ends of the radius and the ulna. "Nothing too bad," he said. "You won't even need a cast. A plastic brace for a while, then tight wrappings, and you'll be as good as new. So long as you take it easy on that wrist," he added.

"How easy?" Stevie asked Nurse Wheldon, Dr. Weaver's assistant, while being fitted with the plastic wrist brace. "Can I ride?"

Nurse Wheldon had been poking Stevie with needles and looking at her tongue and throat and stitching her up and holding her hand during worse for as long as Stevie could remember, years longer than Dr. Weaver. The woman had worked for Dr. Bartins before he retired and Dr. Weaver took over. Every year of her life, Stevie had come to see Nurse Wheldon. Except the past year.

"Not right away," Nurse Wheldon said. She tugged the Velcro straps into place, securing the brace. "But you'll have to ask the doctor."

Stevie looked away. She had already asked. His answer had been, "Not for the first couple weeks." Two weeks was too long, with her next race coming in less than four.

"How did you hurt it?" Dr. Weaver had asked.

"While riding," Stevie said. "It just... started hurting. I first noticed it in the second turn, but then it got worse—a lot worse—in the last turn. Maybe I pulled on the reins too hard," she added, offering the possibility to both the doctor and herself.

"You didn't fall off? Or hit it against anything?"

Stevie shook her head. "No."

"Interesting." Dr. Weaver looked thoughtful. "That's not what I would've expected. Well, not from just holding the reins."

"What were you expecting?" Stevie asked.

"Gymnastics, maybe. A fall out of the saddle."

"I didn't fall out of the saddle. I'm a *Buckbee*."

The doctor shrugged, and gave her a lopsided grin. "What do I know? I'd never seen any horse-related injuries at all before I moved here."

"So maybe I'll be able to ride sooner than two weeks?"

Then he shook his head, the grin disappearing. "No, I don't think so. If it was riding that caused the strain, that's what you need to avoid for it to start healing. I know that's not what you want to hear," he said, holding up a hand to stop Stevie's protest, "but that's the way it has to be. This is a serious injury, and you need to treat it seriously for it to heal properly."

"What about normal work?" Blake asked. "Can she still do her chores around the ranch?"

"Avoid anything that puts stress on that wrist," Dr. Weaver said. "No heavy lifting or pulling, for example. She's not totally disabled, of course. She just needs to be careful."

"Careful?" Blake asked. "Stevie?"

"Oh shut up," Stevie said and hit him on the back of his head with her hard plastic brace. It hurt her wrist, but the solid *Thunk!* and Blake's surprised *Hey!* were worth it.

When they returned from the doctor, Dad didn't say anything. His eyes took in the brace on Stevie's wrist, and Stevie could tell he was estimating the cost. Two doctor's visits in the same day, one for a troublesome horse, the other for a troublesome daughter. She expected him to say something, maybe yell at her to be more careful. But he didn't say anything. He just grunted and shook his head.

Unable to use a shovel, push a mower, or lift a saddle, Stevie found herself relegated to the house to clean the kitchen. "But it's not my day to clean," she protested. "Or cook."

"You're no use to me out here," Blake said. "Might as well be of use somewhere. And," he added, "I don't want to find you just watching TV. Or yakking on the phone."

"Yes, mother dear," she said. "Whatever you say, mother dear."

That lasted three days. Even watching TV in the morning and the afternoon, and sitting on the fence watching the horses when she could, by Thursday the house was cleaner than she ever remembered it being. Certainly cleaner than she had ever made it. She had gone through the kitchen, the pantry, both bathrooms, the family room, and her own room. She had even read two complete books, after dinner, sitting on the front porch in the late evening before the sun went down.

Wednesday night, closing the book on her lap and looking at the last pink clouds of the sunset, Stevie realized that she had never thought of how much work it took to keep the ranch going. And she had been gone nearly a year. No wonder Blake wanted to go to college. How had he even had time to date Shannon before Stevie got back?

And how would she and Dad replace Blake? Would Dad really send her to Tulsa for the school year again? What would happen to the ranch then?

Last summer, she had done her chores grudgingly—except where it meant being with the horses—sometimes skipping the chores altogether to ride on Rain and Buckaroo and the other horses or to go into town and be with Michelle and Lisa Evans and Latonya Cummings. And she had had fewer chores then, because she and Edwin had split the drudge work that Dad and Blake didn't want.

If Edwin were still—still *here*, she thought, not wanting to think of why he was gone—then maybe Blake going away wouldn't be such a big deal. But Edwin had been—gone—for almost a year now. And Blake would be off to college and impossibly far away all too soon.

What would she and Dad do then? What *could* they do?

The pink faded into the dark blue of night as Stevie thought about that. She came to no useful conclusion.

Thursday morning Dad found her in his office. She was on the phone, talking to Michelle as she re-arranged the books on his shelves, with the TV loud enough to be heard from the living room.

Stevie gave him a smile and continued with her sorting. She hadn't expected to enjoy the housework as much as she did. It wasn't the work itself—and certainly not the cooking; she had fixed Hamburger Helper every night, hoping that she would be relieved of that duty—but it was nice to work on her own, not taking orders from Blake or Dad. Just doing what needed to be done. She tried to explain to Michelle.

"The domestication of Stevie Buckbee," Michelle said. "Getting you ready to be a loving wife."

"As if," Stevie said. She picked up the next book, checked the title and moved it to the proper shelf. "I just never thought of it as anything but *work* before. Unwanted work. Now, though—"

"That's what I said," Michelle said, "you *want* to do the work. That's what 'domesticated' *means*, dear. Travis will be so pleased—"

"Whatever." Every conversation with Michelle came around to Travis sooner or later. This one had already included Travis twice. "You've seen Travis more than I have this week. I haven't seen him since the race—" Stevie knew it was the wrong thing to say as soon as she said it.

"Do you want me to tell him you miss him?" Michelle asked.

"Michelle!"

"Stevie!"

Stevie heard Dad's voice and looked at him again. He was talking, and pointing to the front door, but with the TV in one ear and Michelle in the other, he was drowned out. "Hang on," she said into the phone, then held it to her chest. "What?" she asked, almost shouting.

Dad seemed to repeat whatever he had said before. Stevie wasn't sure, though. Gunshots and shouting police from a commercial for a new crime drama overwhelmed Dad's voice. Dad finished by pointing even more emphatically at the front door.

"What?" Stevie asked again.

Dad looked annoyed now. He rolled his eyes, and then

hooked his finger at her, telling her to come closer.

Stevie put the book she held back on its shelf and walked over to Dad. He leaned over her, pointed to the front door, and said, his voice loud enough now that Stevie knew she could have heard him even if she had stayed across the room, "Get. Out!"

"I'm cleaning," Stevie said. "I'm sorting your books—"

"Out!" Dad repeated.

Stevie looked into Dad's eyes, trying to gauge how angry he really was. Or if he was angry at all. She had put off cleaning his office, because he didn't like it when she went in there. Was he angry about that? She wasn't sure, but he might've been suppressing a smile.

"This is the last room to clean," Stevie said. "I'm not *touching* Blake's room—"

"Out," Dad said. Now he wasn't shouting, but he was just as emphatic.

"Fine," Stevie said. "I'm out, I'm out. No need to say 'Thank you' or anything." She stepped around Dad and went into the living room.

The TV cut off as she put the phone to her ear again, startling her. Dad had followed her to the living room. He stood there with the remote in one hand, and the other hand still pointing to the front door.

"All the way out," Dad said. "The house is clean enough." Stevie opened her mouth to protest, but Dad wasn't finished. "I just want it quiet again, for a few hours."

Stevie stopped her protest, realizing what she would be protesting, and closed her mouth before it could say anything counterproductive. "Can I go over to see Michelle?" she asked after a second.

"Just let Blake know where you've gone," Dad said, then he headed into the kitchen.

Friday morning, without thinking about it, Stevie left her brace in her room. The pain had been less each day. This morning, like every morning, she had removed the wrist brace to take her shower. After her shower, though, she forgot to put the brace back on. Blake noticed it at breakfast.

"Maybe I don't need it anymore," Stevie said. She flexed her wrist, spinning her hand around. She stirred up only the slightest ache. The grinding pain from Monday was gone. "It barely hurts at all. Maybe I can ride again?"

"Don't be stupid," Blake said. "The doctor said it would be two weeks before you should even think about riding."

"But— Look." Stevie rotated her wrist in the opposite direction. "The doctor's wrong. I'm almost healed."

"Almost isn't good enough," Blake said. "But if you are almost healed, I'm going to feel a bit stupid."

"You *are* stupid."

"Shut up. I meant, like maybe I should've waited before hiring extra help."

"You hired someone?"

"Oh. So you weren't mouthing off? Just mindlessly repeating what I say?" Stevie stuck her tongue out as Blake continued. "There's too much that needs to be done. And it looked like you were going to be useless for almost a month."

"I'm not useless. Done for what?"

Blake looked down at his bowl of cereal and spooned in a mouthful. "To get this place cleaned up and presentable again," he said, talking around the food in his mouth. "I figured we would need help before the end of summer, anyway. Your hurting yourself only made it happen sooner."

"I didn't hurt myself— Does Dad know?"

"Dad knows I hired someone, yeah. He's the one with the checkbook."

"So who is it?"

Blake stopped talking then. He pushed another spoonful of cereal into his mouth.

"Who is it?" she asked again.

Blake looked up and grinned at her, showing milk and cereal in his teeth.

"Gross," she said, but didn't look away. "Who?"

"Cheap, underpaid, underage labor," Blake said, his mouth still full. He chewed, swallowed and added, "Don't worry about it. You'll like him."

Stevie looked at him through slitted eyes. "Like who?"

Stevie pushed open the front door and stepped out onto the porch. She used her left hand to open the door. Blake had made her put the brace back on, but she didn't think she needed it. She noticed no pain at all opening the door. "You didn't need to hire anyone," she said again.

Blake followed her outside. "Yes, I did."

"I can work again—"

"Good. You can mow the lawn while we get to work on the practice pen."

"I don't want to *mow*—"

"Neither do I," Blake said, flashing a smug smile at her. "And I'm not going to *pay* someone to do it." Stevie opened her mouth to protest again, but Blake held up his hand. "You want to help," he said, "that's what you're going to do."

Stevie decided to let it pass. "So how about riding?" she asked. "If I can work, I can ride."

"No," Blake said, his voice firm. "I'm not willing to risk it yet. Let's wait until Doc Weaver checks you out again on Monday."

Stevie wanted to argue the point further, but Blake waved at someone behind her. "Hey, Travis."

Stevie turned to see Travis Delozier walking up the driveway. Travis nodded and waved back. She turned back to Blake. "What's he doing here?"

"I told him to be here at eight," Blake said.

Stevie looked over her shoulder at Travis, then glared at Blake. "You hired Travis?"

Blake grinned. "I told you you'd like him."

Stevie tried to hit him with her brace, but he dodged this time.

* * *

Still, Stevie thought, it felt good to be working outside again, where the breeze carried the scent of the ranch, the mixed smells of cut grass and manure and horses. The brace reminded her to be careful. When she would push down on the mower to prop up the front wheels and turn it around, though, Stevie noticed her wrist less than she noticed Blake and Travis working around the practice pen. And that interfered with her enjoyment.

Being able to use the practice pen again would be good. Hiring Travis Delozier to help out—

Michelle was going to have a field day with *that*. Stevie tried not to think about either Travis or Michelle.

After lunch, when she had finished mowing the lawn around the house, Stevie helped Blake and Travis as best she could, lifting and carrying tools and dragging spools of wire with just her right hand. She started to push the loaded wheelbarrow, but Blake glared at her and Travis took it from her.

Feeling excluded, she left the two of them working and went to the northeast pasture. She found the horses bunched around the pasture's south fence, standing in what shade was there from the trees outside the fence.

Jack Rabbit nickered at her, as did Buckaroo. Stevie smiled and waved at both of them. Rain nickered, as well, but Stevie ignored her. The other horses just looked at Stevie, nodded, then went back to grazing and swishing.

Jack Rabbit stood in the heart of the shade. He had been standing still when Stevie walked up, but now, as she started to walk toward him, he pranced, and then trotted out to the middle of the field.

Stevie turned to watch him run, and felt the urge to run alongside him. She could almost feel the rush of wind across her face and through her hair.

But she didn't run. She smiled and kept her face to him as he ran a full circle around her. When he had come back to his place in the shade, he blew and pranced some more, letting her know he was happy to see her, and asking if they would ride today.

Stevie shook her head. "Not yet, boy," she said. "Sorry." She walked up to him and stroked his neck with her right hand and offered him a treat from her pocket with her left hand.

As he had all week, Jack Rabbit sniffed at the brace, not liking it.

"I don't like it either," she said.

Jack Rabbit overcame his dislike of the brace and took the treat off her hand with his teeth. He crunched the treat, then sniffed at her pocket for another one.

Stevie laughed, then pulled out another treat and gave it to him. She stroked his neck some more, then walked to the fence and leaned against it.

As Buckaroo and a few of the other horses gathered around Stevie, also wanting treats, Jack Rabbit took the opportunity to once again tell his story of the race. He danced in place, his hoofs sending up dust clouds, calling to mind the dirt of the arena. He shifted his haunches as the mental images he projected showed him coming tight around the barrels. He finished with a whinny and a partial rear, head up, left foreleg up, and looking at the east horizon.

Stevie applauded his performance, as she had every day this week. And she laughed. Because with each "telling", the race became faster, the turns around the barrels tighter and smoother, and the final charge to the gate that much more of a blur.

The other horses only glanced at Jack Rabbit briefly, then were nosing Stevie again, looking for treats. Satchmo, further down the fence, not part of the group around Jack Rabbit and Stevie, snorted and turned his back. Rain stood outside the group. She tried to meet Stevie's eyes, but Stevie wouldn't look at her.

* * *

She came back to the practice pen at the peak of the afternoon heat. Both Blake and Travis had their shirts off now,
sweat and dirt outlining the muscles of their arms and chests
and backs. Stevie looked away, feeling a flush in her cheeks.
And then felt embarrassed that she felt embarrassed. She
had grown up around men and boys who worked shirtless
and it never bothered her. Except when she was younger,
and not understanding, had wanted to take her shirt off
too—

Thinking of that now, just as Travis looked at her, made
the heat in her cheeks flare even more.

"There you are," Blake said. "Can you get us some
Gatorades from the fridge?"

When she came out with the cold plastic bottles, which
quickly beaded with condensation in the humid air, Blake
and Travis were using their shirts as towels, pushing the
sweat off their faces. They hung their shirts around their
necks as Stevie handed them their drinks. She tried not to
look at either of them. Especially Travis.

Blake took his drink and headed toward the house. "I'll
be back in a few minutes," he said.

"If you were going in anyway," Stevie said to his back,
embarrassment giving way to annoyance, "you could've
got the Gatorade yourself."

Blake turned around, walking backward, and just smiled
at her. Before she could do more than give him an annoyed
look, he spun the rest of the way around and went up the
steps and into the house.

Stevie stuck her tongue out. Probably going to call
Shannon or something else equally stupid.

"How did you hurt your wrist?" Travis asked.

Stevie turned back to face Travis. The question surprised
her. Then she remembered that she hadn't spoken to him
in over a week. She met Travis's eyes only briefly, then
looked down at her wrist, her cheeks getting warm again.
She could also feel her arm sweating inside the brace, and
suddenly worried that she would have a tan line because of

it. "I'm not sure," she said. She flexed the wrist experimentally, rotating her hand back and forth within the limits of the brace, confirming yet again that the injury seemed to have healed.

"Were you running with the horses again?"

Stevie looked over at the house. Had Blake come back out? Or Dad? The dark shadows of the porch were empty, though. No one stood there, or sat on the swing. No one else was there to hear his question. She breathed a sigh of relief.

When she looked at Travis again, he was pulling on his t-shirt. "No," she said, and looked away. "We... I...," she started. Her wrist twinged with pain and for an instant she was back at the race. Her and Jack Rabbit, girl and horse almost as one, coming around the second barrel, their combined left foreleg coming down hard on the earth of the arena. She shook her head to clear out the images, and the lingering pain. "It was at the race."

"Did you fall off?" Travis asked as he pushed his head through. The neck of the shirt pressed his sweaty and disheveled hair against his scalp, and pulled it away from his face except for one thick lock that hung over his left eye.

"No," Stevie said, simultaneously resisting the urge to push the lock of hair out of his eye—and to hit him upside the head with her brace. "I didn't fall off. I'm not an infant."

Travis shrugged and took a long gulp of his Gatorade. The movement of his Adam's apple, bobbing up and down as he drank, caught Stevie's eye. He saw her watching him and stopped drinking with a cough.

"Just forget it," she said, suppressing a laugh. "It's almost healed anyway."

"Good," Travis said, wiping his mouth with the back of his hand. He looked at Stevie, then past her to the house. "Is it OK if I sit on the porch?"

"Of course. That's what it's for."

Travis sat on the swing. He left enough room she could've sat down beside him, but Stevie took a place on the porch railing, beside the swing, where she could lean back against the house and look out at the ranch. The air conditioner compressor around the corner of the house started up with a whine and its fan drowned out the sounds of the countryside.

"Do you miss him?" Travis asked after a few minutes.

Stevie looked at Travis. He wasn't looking at her. He faced the ranch, but he wasn't looking at that either. His eyes seemed to be focused past the porch, past the ranch, past everything. She whispered the question, "Edwin?"

Travis nodded.

"Yeah," Stevie said. "I've missed him a lot the last few weeks."

"Me too." Travis seemed about to say more, so Stevie didn't turn away. She wasn't sure how many minutes passed before Travis said, "I'm sorry."

"It wasn't your fault," Stevie said.

"Wasn't it?"

His answer shocked Stevie. She shook her head. "No. It wasn't." *It was your mother's.* She almost said it, but stopped herself.

Travis looked at her now, as if he had heard the words she didn't say, and Stevie looked away, ashamed of herself for even thinking them. "It was nobody's fault," she said.

Travis didn't say anything for a while. "If we had just..." He paused and sighed. "I just wish he were here."

Stevie brought her gaze back to him. He still looked at her. She felt tears in her eyes. Because she missed Edwin, and because Travis's eyes were dry. "Me too."

"You're a lot like him. In some ways," he added before Stevie could protest. "Prettier, of course."

Stevie turned her head, as much to protest the compliment as to hide the new warmth in her cheeks.

"Sometimes, when you laugh, I can hear him."

She stopped a sobbed that welled up in her chest, and used the knuckles of her right hand to push away the tears in her eyes. But she didn't look at Travis again. She didn't want him to see her crying. She didn't know why, but it just seemed... too intimate. Travis wasn't her friend. He was Edwin's. And because Travis wasn't crying. So she swung her legs over the railing and jumped down from the porch.

The air conditioner stopped, its fan spinning to a halt, and the silence—made even emptier because she could feel Edwin's absence—seemed to press against her.

"I'm sorry." Travis's voice was just a hoarse whisper but she heard him clearly.

As she walked away, crying, she didn't turn back to face Travis. She just shook her head. She didn't want him to see her. And she didn't want to see the pain in his face that she heard in his voice. She didn't think she could take it.

Travis caught up to her in the northeast pasture where she finally stopped. The horses had perked up to see her again so soon, but had hung back, unsure in the face of her emotions. Only Rain had ventured forward, but Stevie had turned her back on the old mare, and had seen Travis walking toward her, as unsure as the horses.

He stopped a pace away, just out of reach. "I'm sorry, Stevie," Travis said. "I didn't want to make you cry."

Stevie pushed the tears out of her eyes again, then met Travis's gaze head on. His eyes showed his pain, but there were still no tears. Just like Dad.

"You're so *stupid*," Stevie said, to Travis and maybe to Dad too. She tried not to shout it when she said it again. "You're so stupid. You didn't make me cry. Did you think you're the only one that misses Edwin? Did you? And... and..." She paused to take a breath. "And it's not your fault. Don't ever say that again."

Travis didn't answer, just looked back at her.

The sound of Blake calling their names pulled their attention back to the ranch. Stevie wiped her eyes again and sniffed. She headed back toward the house, stepping past Travis, and not looking at him, and trying not to remember he had called her pretty. Probably just further proof of how stupid he could be.

Chapter 9
Arguments

On Monday, Dr. Weaver looked back and forth from the x-ray of Stevie's wrist taken a week before, and the x-ray he had just done. He shook his head. "Amazing," he said. "Maybe I've underestimated the benefits of country living."

Stevie didn't know about country living being all that great, except as it related to horses. So she cut to the important part. "Does that mean I can ride?" she asked.

"Hmm?" The doctor looked at her, as if he had forgotten she was there. "Oh, yes, I can't see any reason why not." He looked back at the x-rays and said something else Stevie didn't catch. Because she wasn't listening.

"Yes!" Stevie said, and slid down off the examination bench, landing so that the heels of her boots clacked loudly on the tile floor. "Seeya, Doc."

She left the wrist brace on the bench and pushed out into the waiting room where Blake sat reading an old issue of *Sports Illustrated*. "Ha!" she said loudly. "Riding lessons. Tonight. Be there. No more running away from your responsibilities, Blake Buckbee."

Blake looked up, a surprised look—and maybe even a hurt look—mixing with open rebellion in his face. "Running away?" he asked. Something in his voice made Stevie's smile falter. "Is that what I've been doing?"

135

"What's gotten into you?" she asked. Blake just looked at her, so she went on. "You can ask the doctor yourself, if you want." She pointed back to the examination room.

"I will." Blake put the magazine down and stood up. He walked past Stevie, leaving her alone in the waiting room. He came out a couple minutes later, carrying her wrist brace.

Stevie greeted him with a smug look. "See? I told you he said I could ride."

"Yes, he said you can ride. But he's a doctor. What does he know about riding?"

Taken aback, Stevie stared at him. "What?"

"Nothing. Here," he said, tossing the brace at her as he walked past.

She caught the brace, and held it away from her in distaste. "What's this for?"

"We paid for it," Blake said. "Might as well keep it." He reached the office door, opened it, and looked back at her. "You coming?" He didn't wait for her, forcing Stevie to rush to catch up.

In the truck, pulling into the early morning traffic of downtown Antlers, Stevie asked, "What's up with you?" Blake hadn't said anything else to her. The tight muscles of his jaw reminded her of Dad. And his silence.

Blake gave her only a brief look before focusing on the street again. "Nothing's up with me. I'm glad your wrist is better."

They rode home with nothing more said. Stevie wanted to talk about the riding lessons, but Blake's mood made her decide not to push it. She had been thinking over the weekend, though, replaying the race in her mind, and she realized that everyone was right. She had screwed up the turns. More specifically, the lead changes. She had to admit that much, if only to herself. And that it was her being wrong that had—somehow—hurt her wrist. Jack Rabbit had been able to make those impossible turns because—? She didn't know.

The loud ratcheting sound of Blake setting the emergency brake after parking in front of the house brought her back to the present. Stevie found she was holding her left wrist in her right hand, massaging it. She looked at Blake and saw him watching her.

She let go of her wrist. "It doesn't hurt," she said. "Just a habit..." Blake didn't seem interested, so she trailed off.

"I'm not running away," he said. "You know that, don't you?"

"What?"

"I'm not running away," he repeated. "From you. From Dad. Or from the ranch."

"Who—" *Who said anything about that?* she started to ask. But then she saw Dad come out of the house and stand on the porch, waiting for them, waiting for the doctor's report. And she remembered Dad's voice, yelling at Blake, accusing him of exactly that. *Isn't that what you're doing, Blake? Giving up? Quitting? Running away?* "I know," she said. She wanted to stop there. But her mouth kept going. "But you're going to be so far away. Couldn't you go to college at Southeastern? That's where Michelle's brother is going."

Blake sighed and shook his head. "No," he said. "Forget it." And he got out of the truck.

Over the next week, with Blake and Travis and Stevie working long days, the ranch transformed, becoming much closer to the picture-perfect memory that Stevie had from her earliest childhood. Except that Edwin and Mom were still gone. And Dad seemed to pull more into himself.

Like the week before, Dad had risen early to be awake when the vet came by to check out Jack Rabbit again—and give Jack Rabbit a clean bill health once again—but after that, Dad was never up and about before Stevie and Blake. They and Travis had been working at least an hour before they saw Dad.

Dad worked around them sometimes, doing the day-to-day chores of the ranch, feeding and grooming the horses, leading the horses from one pasture to another, dealing with the few remaining stabling clients that came by to see their horses. But he never worked with Stevie and Blake and Travis. He smiled and talked with the clients and helped their children if they needed assistance with saddling or leading their horses into trailers. But he spoke very little to Stevie, seldom spoke to Blake without a "Damn it" or worse, and never spoke to Travis at all.

Dinners were quiet, unless Stevie said something. Which she did sometimes just to cut through the silence between the two men across the table from her. But their terse answers to her, and unwillingness to discuss in front of her whatever it was they were conspicuously not arguing about made her fall quiet as well.

During her riding lessons after dinner, under the still-bright summer sky, the tension—with Dad, anyway—would seem disappear, and Blake was his normal self. More than once Stevie asked, "What's wrong with Dad?"

A dark look would pass over Blake's face when she asked that, but he would only say, "He doesn't like what we're doing."

"Cleaning up the ranch? He's upset about *that?*"

The look on Blake's face would then become resigned and tired—but also guarded again. "Yeah," he said. When Stevie pressed for more details, he would bring her back to the lesson by pointing out her mistakes.

And she seemed to be making more mistakes than ever.

Amazingly, Blake hadn't been too sarcastic—or too gloating—when she told him about the conclusion she had reached. "I need you to help me fix my lead changes," she had said. Direct, to the point, getting it over with quickly, but already wincing inside.

But Blake just nodded and seemed relieved. By the end of the week, though, Blake was irritated, she was frustrated, and Jack Rabbit was impatient.

"Why aren't you *listening* to me?" Blake shouted at her. "Watch me." He put Satchmo into a slow trot and took him around the barrel, executing the lead change with an ease that only made Stevie more frustrated—and made Jack Rabbit more sullen.

"I am listening," Stevie said. And she was.

Jack Rabbit wanted to run, wanted to race, and resented being held back. And the horse resisted the changes Stevie tried to make in how they took the turns around the barrels. Jack Rabbit did better when Blake rode Buckaroo or Rain or one of the other horses. But when Blake rode Satchmo, Jack Rabbit became almost impossible to control.

"Come on, boy," Stevie said, directing Jack Rabbit with the reins, letting him step up to a trot. She settled into the rhythm of his hooves and used her hands on the reins and her legs to change his lead as they continued in a straight line. In her mind she could feel Jack Rabbit's muscles and bones as if they were her own, but she resisted the urge to do as she had during the race and before. She didn't reach into Jack Rabbit. She remained the rider, separate.

She and Jack Rabbit rode back and forth across the pasture, executing lead changes along the straight path. Jack Rabbit made sure Stevie knew that he didn't like it, but he made the changes as she directed. After a half dozen passes, Blake nodded and told her to try it around the barrels again.

Jack Rabbit's resistance returned and they barely walked around the first barrel. The big horse didn't understand why they should change. They had won the race, hadn't they? Stevie sighed, but was too tired after fighting with him all week to explain once again that she was worried about him hurting his legs. And her wrists and ankles.

Jack Rabbit snorted. For the second barrel he asserted himself and cut around it as they had done at the race despite Stevie's protests, and she barely had time to extend herself through him to absorb the shock on his left foreleg.

She bit her lip to keep from crying out at the renewed pain. Blake, though, let loose with a shout of disgust.

"Damn it, Stevie. Keep control of your horse."

Stevie pulled Jack Rabbit around and pointed him to the last barrel, shocked that Blake would say that to her. She felt Jack Rabbit's resistance building, pitting will against will, rider versus horse. Stevie couldn't remember ever feeling so out of place in the saddle. Like she didn't belong there.

As they reached the last barrel, Jack Rabbit planted his hooves. Stevie caught the thought from Jack Rabbit just an instant before he arched his back and bucked. Surprised and hurt that even Jack Rabbit was upset at her, she held on through the buck and the landing, then pushed against the stirrups and pulled back on the reins, trying to regain control, trying to keep his head up. She could feel the pain in his cheeks at the pressure of the bit, but he pulled against it, wanting to buck again.

"Whoa, boy," Stevie said, maintaining the pressure. "Calm down, boy."

Jack Rabbit relented, but let her know that he was tired of this nonsense. Tired of having to follow Satchmo. Tired of walking and trotting when he wanted to run. When he wanted to *race*.

"I know," she said. "I know. Me too. But we have to..."

Jack Rabbit shook his head and blew out a loud breath. He didn't want to listen.

Blake came up alongside on Satchmo, concern and consternation in his voice as he said, "That's enough for today, I think. Lead him back to the barn."

Stevie nodded. "OK. But I'll ride him back."

"No," Blake said. "Lead him." He flicked the reins and Satchmo carried him away toward the gate before Stevie could protest.

Sighing, wondering if Travis would be snapping at her next—he was the only one who hadn't yelled at her today—Stevie swung her leg over and stepped down. Her left wrist gave her a twinge of pain, but it wasn't enough to hinder her. "We need to learn how to do this, boy," she said, stroking Jack Rabbit's neck. Jack Rabbit turned his head and didn't look at her. When she led him, though, he followed.

Through the next week, Jack Rabbit continued to resist her. Blake got angry with her, thinking she was the one being stubborn, sounding more and more like Dad when he lost his patience. She was stubborn about refusing to ride Rain in practice when he insisted, but she was able to prove to him that she had been listening when she rode Buckaroo.

She hadn't ridden Buckaroo in over a year. The aging gelding carried her with pride, happier than she had seen him in a while, pleased with himself that she had agreed to ride him. And he responded to her direction as she rode, coming around the barrels with flawless—if slow—turns.

"OK, so it's not you," Blake admitted.

Stevie sat in the saddle and stroked Buckaroo's neck. He almost purred, and shuffled just a bit, a restrained dance.

"Are you sure—" Blake started.

"Yes," Stevie said, cutting him off. She knew what he was going to ask. Again. "I'm riding Jack Rabbit in the race. We're a team."

"You're not much of a team at the moment."

"He's a good horse. He'll learn. We're both learning."

"Alright. Just take Buckaroo around the barrels again. Go as fast as you feel comfortable."

Buckaroo leaped into the run, and his joy at the chance made Stevie laugh as they rode along. They went around the barrels, cutting the turns with a pocket of six feet, kicking up dust, both of them working together to cross the finish line where Blake stood with his watch.

After they had reined to a stop, Blake walked up and patted Buckaroo on the neck, ruffling his mane. "Good job," he said. "Both of you." Buckaroo held his head up and pranced in place.

"How'd we do?" Stevie asked.

"Twenty-two seconds. Respectable," Blake added when Buckaroo seemed disappointed, the horse dipping his head.

Stevie nodded and stroked Buckaroo's neck and mane. "Absolutely."

Buckaroo appreciated the praise and perked his ears. He didn't know math, but he knew he was old and Jack Rabbit was young and he made sure that Stevie knew he was happy for the chance to charge the barrels again.

Stevie climbed down and gave Buckaroo a tight hug around the neck. As she breathed in the smell of him, scents of horse and leather and grass and dirt, she caught an image from him, a memory. Of Buckaroo and Mom racing around the barrels in an open field. Blue sky and green grass and white barrels, everything blurring together in the wind of their passage. Stevie hugged him tighter. "You did good, boy."

The day of the race started badly, a fitting follow up to a bad week. Stevie only rode Jack Rabbit that week, but the horse resented her praise of Buckaroo, and became even more frustrated with the slow pace of their workouts.

"We're saving you for the race," Stevie tried to explain. "You'll get to run as fast as you want on Saturday."

But Jack Rabbit pretended to ignore her. Worse, he tried to buck her off twice during that week, both times as they went into turns. The second time caught Stevie off guard, and she lost her grip on the reins. She kept her balance, though, gripping with her legs, and was able to slip off after the first buck, and get under Jack Rabbit's head, out of reach of his back hooves.

Talking fast, trying to calm Jack Rabbit down with the sound of her voice and assurances that he would be able to race soon and they would win again, Stevie looked over at Blake. She expected a reprimand, or maybe another threat to keep them out of the race. But Blake only shook his head, his frustration as plain to her as Jack Rabbit's.

"Get back in the saddle," he said, "and try it again."

Stevie did. That had been Wednesday.

Jack Rabbit's mood hadn't improved the rest of the week, and even on Saturday, the day of the race, he remained sullen and uncooperative. He pulled his head back from her, forcing Stevie to use a stool to get his halter on, and tried to pull his legs and hooves out of her grip as she groomed him. Then he refused to be led into the trailer until Stevie had worked him in the corral, leading him back and forth for over twenty minutes.

"It'll be OK, boy," she said. She moved her hand to stroke his nose once she had him secured in the trailer. Jack Rabbit moved his head away from her hand, not looking at her, as much as he could. He couldn't move far enough, but his reaction stopped her. She stroked his neck instead. "Come on, Jack Rabbit. You wanted to race. And in a few hours..." Her voice drifted off into a sigh.

"We can do it, boy," she went on after a few quiet seconds. "Together. You and I." She thought of the first race, picturing their speed and the hearing again the sounds of the crowd and the announcer giving their time. *16:68.* "We can do it."

Jack Rabbit looked at her now, and he replayed his memory of the race for her, shifting in his restraints.

"Exactly," Stevie said. She went on tiptoe and kissed the bridge of his nose. "Let's go race."

"20.17 seconds," the announcer said, as the digits flashed on the scoreboard.

Stevie tried not to cry as she directed Jack Rabbit out of the arena. Jack Rabbit jerked against the reins. He didn't want to cry. He wanted to do the race again. And do it *right* this time. Do it so they *won.* The horse didn't know clocks or seconds or timings. But he knew they hadn't won. And he blamed Stevie.

Stevie understood. She blamed herself too.

"Good job," Blake said. He wasn't smiling, but he did look satisfied.

Stevie turned her head so he wouldn't see the tears. She just nodded, because she didn't trust her voice. Jack Rabbit snorted and stamped a hoof down, expressing his disagreement with Blake. Stevie—doing what Blake had told her—had held him back, slowed him down. Jack Rabbit's thoughts and feelings weren't in words, more a rush of images and emotions, but Stevie heard them like an accusation in her mind.

"You did the turns exactly right," Blake went on. "I'm sorry you didn't win, but—"

"We didn't even *place*," Stevie said.

"It's not just about winning," Blake said. "And you looked really good out there. Like a professional—"

"In slow motion replay, maybe." She shoved the tears out of her eyes with a knuckle, then pulled her leg over and stepped out of the saddle.

"No. You looked..."

Jack Rabbit pulled against the reins she held. Stevie snapped the reins and glared at Blake. "What? What did I look like? A loser?"

Blake wasn't looking at her. He had turned to look back the way she had come, back into the arena. "You looked like Mom," he said.

"Great," Stevie said. "So I did look like a loser." She yanked on the reins and led Jack Rabbit back to the trailer.

"Mom was a great rider," Blake said behind her.

"Yeah," she said. "And then she rode right out of our lives." She turned to glare back at Blake. "Don't you get it? I don't *want* to be like Mom."

"Stevie," Blake called after her, but she kept walking.

At least the ranch looked good, Stevie thought as Blake drove the truck and trailer through the front gate. Her summer of barrel racing was half over. Or maybe it was all over. At the very least it was falling down and looking like it might not recover, torn apart by Blake's trying to make her ride like... like... she didn't even want to think about that. Trying to make her ride Rain. Or Buckaroo. Or some other broken down horse. Trying to make her lose. And by Jack Rabbit pulling away from her with his single-minded focus on winning.

She saw Dad standing on the front porch, waiting for them. And reminding Stevie of all the other ways the summer she had planned so meticulously had been screwed up. From those first few days, when Dad hadn't come to pick her up in Tulsa, through his late daily starts and sullen moods and continued drinking and... And not going to see her race.

Looking away from Dad even as Blake pointed the truck right at him, coming to a stop, her eyes swung over the ranch again, the barn, the corral and pastures, the practice pen. The pasture fences still showed visible signs of disrepair, and further out the weeds were still there, growing tall. But near the house, and even the house itself, looked better than it had in years.

It almost looked like home again.

"Yeah," Blake said. "It's looking really good."

His voice startled her. She didn't realize she had spoken.

"We still have a lot to do," Blake went on, opening his door. "The real estate agent will be here on Friday, though, and I want the barn painted by then."

Stevie had her mouth open to ask—or yell—*Real estate agent?* But Blake shut his door before she could get out anything but a choked, angry sound.

She grabbed the handle of her own door and pushed out of the truck, jumping down and coming around the still open door fast enough to grab Blake's elbow before he made it halfway up the steps to the porch. She saw Dad's mouth open in surprise, or maybe to ask her how the race went, but she didn't wait to hear what he had to say. "What real estate agent?"

Blake pulled his elbow out of her grip. "Allison Keenan," he said. "You know her."

Stevie stared at him. "What does my knowing her have to do with anything? Why is she coming?"

Blake looked down at her. He stood on the middle step. Behind him, on the porch, Dad looked down at her too. Stevie shifted her attention to Dad. "Why is there a real estate agent coming?"

Dad looked away without answering.

"We're selling the ranch," Blake said.

Stevie looked at Blake, then back at Dad. Dad wouldn't meet her eye. He looked past both her and Blake, at the corral and the pasture beyond.

She backed up, away from Blake, away from Dad. "No."

Blake met her eyes. "We don't have any choice—"

"No!" Stevie shouted and spun around, refusing to look at Blake. Or at Dad. She might have run away—to the horses, to Michelle, to anywhere but here—but the truck blocked her way. In the windshield of the truck she could see the roof of the house, the gables pointing up at the clear blue sky, both gables and sky stretched by the curve of the glass making her feel even smaller.

"Stevie," Blake said. "It's for the best."

"It's that why we've been cleaning up the ranch?" Stevie asked. She felt sick. "Not so we could live here? But so we could *leave*?" Stevie turned back to face Blake. He no longer stood on the steps. He faced her at her level. Dad still stood on the porch, though. He looked down at her, returning her gaze now, but didn't speak. "Why won't you *say* something?" she shouted at Dad. "Tell him we're not selling the ranch. Tell him!"

Dad sighed, but only shook his head.

Frustration and panic choked her, and she could only get out, "Please?" Tears made it hard to make out Dad's expression.

"You and Dad can't run the whole ranch by yourselves, Stevie."

"Me and Dad?" Stevie turned on Blake. Anger beat back the panic and dried her eyes. "Me and Dad wouldn't *have* to," she said, "if you weren't running away." The words came out before she could stop them. But she didn't take them back. "You can't sell the ranch. This is our *home*. We *live* here."

The muscles of Blake's jaw tightened. "I'm trying," he said, his voice low and controlled, in contrast to Stevie, and very different from what Stevie could see in his eyes, "to do what's best for you—"

"For me? This isn't what's best for me."

"For all of us," Blake insisted.

"For *you*, you mean." She could see that hurt him. But that only made her bolder. "So you can run away—"

"Stop it." Blake didn't yell, but the tone of his voice, the hard edge made Stevie stop. She couldn't remember him ever using that tone of voice before. She looked at him in surprise, wondering when Blake had become the man who stood in front of her now, the sun hitting him like a spotlight. Dad seemed like a shadow behind him.

"If I was running away," Blake said after a long second, "I would be gone already." With that, he turned around and walked up the steps to the porch.

"No!" Stevie shouted. "You can't just walk away from me." She stood her ground, but Blake didn't turn around. "It's no wonder Mom left," she yelled at his back. And at Dad, though she didn't look at him. She couldn't look at him. "All the men in her life let her down!"

As Blake walked past Dad, he and Dad looked at each other, but neither spoke. Blake went into the house, opening and closing the glass door, the reflection in the glass, of the barn and the sky and the posts of the porch, hiding him from sight.

Stevie stood there, her mouth hanging open, wishing she could take back the words, trying to think of new words for the emotions that surged through her. Trying to think of what she could say that would make Blake take it back, make him stay. But Blake was gone. She closed her mouth, then opened it again to say something to Dad, who still stood on the porch.

Dad met her eyes.

I didn't mean it, she wanted to say. *Please. You can't sell the farm.* But nothing came out. Because Dad had said nothing. Not a word.

For an instant, she wanted to run to Dad, to hold him while he held her and stroked her hair and told her everything was all right. *Say it*, she wanted to say. *Say that we won't sell the ranch. I'll take it all back if you just say it. Tell me we won't...*

Dad looked away. "No trophy today?" he said.

Stevie stared at him. A sob threatened to burst her heart. "No," she managed to say at last.

Dad looked back at her. "I'm sorry."

"You should be." She didn't even try to stop herself.

Dad winced, and seemed to deflate, as if she had hit him in the stomach. She wanted to run to him. She wanted to run away from him. She wanted him to reassure her. And she could see that he needed her too. But she couldn't go to him. Because when she needed him, he had let her down. Again.

Finally, she turned her back on him and walked away. From him. From Blake. From the house that used to be her home.

Rain stood by the gate as Stevie led Jack Rabbit, groomed and sulky, back to the pasture. The sight of the old mare looking at her, waiting for her, so obviously concerned for her, made the tears well up once again. She had fought the urge to cry while she backed Jack Rabbit out of the trailer, alone, took him to the barn, alone, and groomed him. Alone.

Stevie forced the tears back one more time, pushed the hurt down.

The barn had never seemed so quiet. So empty. Like she had shrunk, withered, and her life was a shell around her. An empty frame of wood with only the scents of hay and horses to remind her of what used to be.

Only Rain waited for her. And for Jack Rabbit. The other horses bunched in the far corner of the pasture.

Stevie opened the gate and led Jack Rabbit through, closed the gate behind them.

Jack Rabbit had sulked through the grooming, not resisting her efforts but not cooperating. He didn't cooperate now either. He stood there, with his head held up, making her reach to remove the halter. When the halter was off, he walked away from her, swishing his tail in dismissal.

She had held him back. She had failed him. He didn't need words for her to understand.

Run with me.

The words in her mind startled Stevie. She looked at Rain, bewildered? Run? Now?

Isn't that what you want to do? Run?

Rain didn't wait for Stevie to reply. She whinnied, like a laugh, and turned and trotted away.

Suddenly Stevie was a child again, watching Mom spin around. The skirt of Mom's dress flared, and Mom laughed. She came to a stop, arms spread wide. Then she smiled and reached down and poked Stevie in the tummy. *Bet you can't beat me to the barn.*

Stevie blinked, and the memory passed. She stood alone—thirteen again, and still in pain—by the pasture gate. Jack Rabbit had joined the rest of the horses. Rain stood about thirty feet away, no longer trotting, looking back at her.

She did want to run. Rain had that right.

But if she started running, Stevie wasn't sure she'd be able to stop.

"Stevie?" Not Rain's voice in her head this time. But not Blake's voice or Dad's either she realized, disappointment stabbing even deeper. Travis stood by the gate.

"Go away, Travis," she said. She turned her face. She didn't want to cry in front of Travis. Not again.

But Travis didn't go away. He climbed over the gate and jumped down. "What's wrong, Stevie?" he asked as he walked over.

Travis stood there, looking at her, just out of arms reach. "Are you OK?" he asked again.

"No, I'm *not* OK," she said. She turned her back on Travis now, pushing the tears out of her eyes and choking back a sob. She didn't know if she could hold herself together. Not when everything was falling apart. But she refused to stop trying. She wouldn't let them sell the farm. She wouldn't let Dad stand there and do nothing. She wouldn't let Blake go away like Edwin had gone and Mom—

Then the tears she had been holding back burst through, and she cried.

She felt Travis's arms around her before she realized he had stepped close. She tried to turn around, to push him away, but his arms had already encircled her, and she ended up with her face against his chest, rubbing her tears into his shirt. She didn't put her arms around him, but she didn't push him away.

When had Travis become so tall? The thought seemed out of place in the turmoil of her mind. She lifted her face to look at him, to ask him when he had become so tall, and his arms so...

His lips touched hers, warm and soft, stopping the question. And stopping her breath. The warmth of the kiss spread across her face and tingled in the nape of her neck and the small of her back where his hands held her. Suddenly she could feel him all the way down her body, her chest, her stomach, her legs, her body against his.

The shock of contact, the electricity of the unexpected kiss, startled her and she pushed him away. His arms resisted the push, but only for a second, then he relented and they separated, still standing close, but no longer touching, just looking at each other.

She looked up at him, into his eyes, and tried to remember what she had been about to ask him. And started to ask him what had just happened. Then she wondered, because of how fast her heart beat and how hard it was to catch her breath, how long they had kissed. But all she managed to say was, "What... ?"

He didn't say anything. If he had smiled, Stevie thought, if he reached for her, she might have kissed him again. But he didn't smile, and his arms remained at his side. He looked away. "I'm sorry," he said.

I'm sorry. Blake had told her that, after the race. And Dad. And now Travis. Everyone was sorry. It was her life they were messing up, but at least they were sorry about it.

"Shut up," she said. She wanted to call him stupid again, but Travis wasn't the one who had been stupid. Who still expected Dad to wake up. Who had listened to Blake tell her how to lose a race. Who had helped Blake clean up the ranch—just so Blake could sell it and take it away from her. Who still wished Mom was there to make her laugh and kiss her where it hurt and make it all better. Even when all of them had let her down, over and over. They were all sorry. But she was the stupid one.

You're being unfair. To them. And to yourself.

"Stop it," Stevie said out loud, spinning to face Rain. "Stop trying to be my mother. You're not her. Your just a broken down old nag. You're just—" She couldn't think of anything else to call Rain, so she shifted her attack. "You're just jealous. Of Jack Rabbit. And me."

"Stevie... ?"

Stevie glared at Rain, for making her look like an idiot. As if she were talking to a horse.

She felt the brush of Rain's mind against hers, saw the beginning of images, but she closed herself.

"No," she told both Rain and Travis. "Just shut up. Just... just leave me alone." She walked away from them, across the pasture, but not to Jack Rabbit and the other horses, who she could see were eyeing her warily, prepared to run away. She walked toward the far fence and the road beyond.

Toward Michelle. Even if the girl *would* wheedle out the part about Travis kissing her. Michelle could sense juicy gossip anywhere within the county and wouldn't relent until she knew all the details. But Michelle would listen, even as she teased Stevie about Travis Delozier—and especially about the kiss. And Michelle wouldn't say she was sorry.

Chapter 10
Hurting

THE WIRE HANDLE of the five-gallon bucket of paint dug into Stevie's palms as she carried it. The weight of the bucket forced her to hunch her shoulders and shuffle, and she could only manage three or four steps before she had to set the bucket down. The first bucket had been easier, though not by much. She took deep breaths, as if she had been running, and massaged the aching red line imprinting deeper and deeper into her palms. Then she picked up the bucket again and pushed forward a few more steps.

Finally, she had the second bucket beside the first, at the foot of the ladder that leaned against the barn. Putting the bucket down for the last time, Stevie stumbled backward and wondered what she was going to do now. Her idea had been simple enough. But with as much trouble as it had been to get the buckets from inside the barn to here, she knew there was no way she would be able to carry one of them up the ladder with her.

Blake could carry the buckets with just his arms bulging. Even Travis seemed to be able to manage the big five-gallon buckets without too much trouble, though with more visible straining than Blake.

Stevie rubbed the palms of her hands, wincing at the pain. It just wasn't fair.

153

Her breathing settled back into its normal rhythm even as her disappointment grew. Her plan had been a good one.

Blake had set her and Travis to painting opposite sides of the barn, then told them he would be back for lunch before driving the truck down the driveway and turning toward town, leaving behind only a small cloud of dust.

The dust hadn't even had time to settle out of the hot, humid July air before Stevie put down the smaller one-gallon bucket and brush Blake had given her and started on her plan. Fifteen minutes later, she stood looking up the length of the ladder to where it leaned against the roof of the barn, and knew she couldn't do it.

Travis came around the back corner of the barn, holding his paintbrush, its bristles bright red from the paint, in one hand and carrying his own one-gallon bucket by its wire handle with his other. Stevie ignored him, and wished he would go away. As she had all week.

"What are you doing?" Travis asked.

"Go away, Travis," she said, still refusing to look at him. Because when she looked at him, ever since that afternoon he kissed her, all she noticed were his eyes and his lips and his hands. And then she would hear—again, as if it just happened—Michelle's squeal of laughter and scandal and her shouting, "Stevie Buckbee's first kiss!" when Stevie finally confessed. And remember the sparkle in Michelle's eyes as she asked, "Did you like it?" And then Stevie's cheeks would get hot. Again.

So it was best not to look at Travis at all.

For a brief moment, Stevie wondered if Travis would carry the buckets up to the roof for her. If she asked him. But she dismissed the idea as soon as it came into her head. She didn't want to ask him. For anything. She didn't want to talk to him. He might—he might stand out of reach and tell her he was sorry again.

"Did you carry those out here by yourself?"

"Of course," Stevie said. "What? Don't you think I'm strong enough?" She sneaked a quick look at his face, to see if he doubted her. Or was impressed. But she couldn't read his face. She just saw his eyes, and his lips as he said something else.

"What for? Why did you bring them out here at all?"

Looking away again, and swallowing, Stevie said, "For nothing. Just go away, Travis."

But Travis didn't go away. She felt him looking at her, then saw him looking at the big buckets. He walked over and set down his bucket, laying the brush across the open top. "Here," he said, and pulled off the tops of the five-gallon buckets. "That should help." He gestured at Stevie's bucket and brush. "You can refill easier that way."

Stevie blinked, and then felt foolish. Of course. The smaller bucket would be much easier to carry up the ladder.

Travis looked at her, his lips and eyes showing a wry smile, then he picked up his bucket and brush and walked away.

"Blake's going to kill you," he said, turning the corner, throwing one last look at her before he went out of sight.

Stevie couldn't stop her smile. "Only if he can catch me," she called after him.

Dad came out of the house, walking stiffly, as she refilled her bucket for the third time. "What the *hell* are you doing?" he shouted.

Stevie turned and smiled at Dad. She pushed her hair out of her eyes, and felt paint smudge across her forehead. She had paint on the back of her hands, and splashed up her forearms and on her legs and shorts and shirt. Paint had overflowed from the big five-gallon bucket the first time she pushed her smaller bucket into the paint to fill it, and wet paint gleamed in puddles in the dirt. She smiled at Dad, and he stopped, as if he began to understand, and he leaned against the corral gate, looking at her.

"I'm painting," Stevie said. "For the real estate agent."

Dad's face contorted, and Stevie knew he was trying not to smile back at her. So she smiled even wider, showing her teeth in a happy, goofy grin. Then she turned to climb the ladder again.

Instead of throwing the paint against the side of the barn, to splatter and dribble down the wooden siding to the dirt of the corral, this time Stevie decided to dump it on the roof. The red paint cascaded across the shingles like a blood tide and spilled over the side or ran down the supports of the ladder.

She turned around to see if Dad was still there. He was, so she gave him another big smile. He smiled back this time. A tight smile with just the corners of his lips drawing up, but still a smile. Then he shook his head and turned to go back into the house.

He paused a few steps away.

"Don't waste too much paint," he said. "Paint costs money." Then he continued on.

Stevie went down the ladder, and decided to switch to the white paint for a few buckets. Just for variety.

By the time Blake came back, the big bucket of red paint had been emptied, and just over half of the white paint was gone too, both colors splattered and dripping all over her side of the barn. She had stopped heaving bucketsful at a time. Now she dipped the paintbrush into the small bucket she carried and flicked droplets of paint at the barn and the fence. She liked the speckle effect.

Blake stopped the pickup with a lurch and a crunch of gravel and got out. He had his mouth open as he stared at Stevie and the barn, but nothing came out.

Stevie smiled at him and waved with her paintbrush. She had even more paint on her skin and clothes and in her hair. She walked from the barn to the corral fence. She figured she must be a sight, and almost told Blake to go get the camera. Michelle would *love* to see—

"What—?" Blake started. As if a cloud passed over the sun, Blake's face became dark and the muscles of his jaw clenched and he stopped. He slammed the door of the truck closed. "God *damn* it, Stevie. What the— What were you *thinking?*"

"I was... ," Stevie said. Her voice trailed off under the force of Blake's eyes. She looked away and pointed with the paintbrush. "Painting," she finished. "I was painting." She risked a look back at Blake. His eyes hadn't budged. She could feel his anger. It seemed to roll off him, adding to the heat of the day, distorting the air around him.

"How could you waste that much paint?"

"I was painting for the real estate agent," Stevie said, finally getting out the punchline. "Don't you think Allison will like—"

"Just shut up." The harshness of his tone stopped Stevie.

Blake looked at her for a few seconds more. Then his eyes took in the spectacle of the barn again, and he spun around, heading for the house.

"I was painting," Stevie shouted at his back. "Isn't this what you wanted?" Blake didn't stop. He went up the steps onto the porch. It was like her voice didn't reach him. She yelled at him even louder. "Stop walking away from me! Why do you think I did this? Because you won't *listen.*"

Blake paused, his hand on the latch of the storm door. He took his hand from the latch, turned around. "You're the one not listening," he said. He had his voice under control, but it carried across to her. "We have to sell—"

"No! We don't!"

Blake shook his head. "You're doing it again—"

"Stop it!" Stevie flung the paintbrush at him. It arced over the corral fence, but didn't come anywhere near Blake. The brush banged against the side of the truck, leaving red and white and pink traces, then fell in the gravel of the driveway. "I don't *want* to sell the ranch. Why should I help you?"

"Ruining the ranch won't help anyone—"

"I'm not the one ruining the ranch."

Blake looked back at her. He didn't say anything for long seconds, and Stevie drew a breath to yell at him some more—

"I'm sorry," Blake said. "You're right."

His admission, and his tone, stopped Stevie, surprised her. She nodded. Of course she was right. But before she could find the words to continue, Blake went on.

"And I'm not ruining it either," he said. "So who do you think that leaves?"

"Hey!" Stevie yelled as Blake turned away from her again. "You can't just—you can just *run away*." She thrust the words at him, knowing they would hurt him.

But Blake ignored her, and went into the house.

Frustrated and furious, Stevie threw her small bucket in the direction of the barn and climbed the corral fence. She wanted to run to the house, to throw open the door so Blake could hear her, and start yelling at him again. She wasn't anywhere *near* finished with him yet. But she didn't run. She kept her control, breathing hard, stomping across to the steps and up the porch. Her feet left paint marks on the first few steps.

"—saw her? You *saw her?*" Blake's voice. "And you didn't stop her? Jesus Christ, Dad, that's almost $200 worth of paint she wasted."

Stevie stopped on the porch, listening.

"Watch your tone, Blake. This is still my ranch—"

"Your ranch? Isn't it a bit late to be—"

"*My* ranch."

"Fine. It's your ranch. Enjoy *your ranch* for the few weeks you have left."

"Blake!"

Stevie had only just enough time to step out of the way of the glass door before Blake stormed out of it. If he saw Stevie, he made no sign of it, striding past her.

"Blake!" she shouted, almost into his ear. "Wait!"

But he didn't stop. She ran down the steps after him, caught his arm before he reached the truck.

"What's going on?" she asked.

Blake looked at her, then brushed her hand off his arm. Red and white paint smudged the skin of his forearm. He looked at the paint, then at her again.

"What's going on?" she asked again.

Behind her, she heard the door open again. "Blake," Dad said.

Blake's eyes focused past Stevie. "Tell her."

Stevie spun around and looked at Dad. He met her eyes, but he didn't say anything. "Tell me what?" She turned to Blake. "Tell me what?"

The men looked at each other, and she looked back and forth, one to the other.

Finally, Dad said, "We have to sell the ranch, Stevie."

The words, spoken quietly, hammered into Stevie and she couldn't breathe. She wanted to protest. She wanted to shout at Dad that he was a liar. He had to be lying. He was finally talking to her, but what he had to say was killing her. She stood there, gasping for air, drowning. She needed Dad to save her, to tell her it wasn't true. But she knew he wouldn't.

"Why?" she managed after a long minute.

Neither Dad nor Blake answered, even though she looked at them both, her eyes pleading for one of them to talk to her.

After what seemed like forever, Blake spoke. "And you call me a coward," he said to Dad. "You accuse me of—" He stopped, turned, and walked away.

Stevie watched Dad watching Blake. She wanted Dad to say something. Anything. To call Blake back. To tell Stevie why they had to sell the ranch. To explain. To apologize. To punish her or praise her. Anything at all.

Behind her she heard Blake yell for Travis, then tell Travis to help him repaint the barn.

Dad met her eyes, then sighed and looked away. He turned his back on her and went back inside the house.

Stevie stood, alone, in the middle of the driveway, crying, while the hot sun dried the red and white paint in her hair and on her skin.

At first she hoped that Dad would come back out. Back to her. But after—she didn't know how long—she pushed the tears out of her eyes and went to help Blake and Travis clean up her mess.

Blake didn't eat dinner with her and Dad that night. Dad fixed dinner, scrambling up sausage and eggs. "Dinner's ready," he called up to Stevie, the only words he had said to her since lunch. And the only words he said while they ate.

The sight of the scrambled eggs and sausage, in the center of the table, still in the skillet used to cook them, took away what little appetite Stevie had. But she ate anyway, mechanically lifting her fork to her mouth, chewing, swallowing. She didn't taste anything. When she finished she went up to her room and resumed trying to brush the paint out of her hair.

She was still there, staring into her mirror, brush in hand, tears from the effort in her eyes—and maybe a few other tears that didn't come from painful brushing—an hour later. Frustrated—with Blake and Dad and the whole universe—she threw the brush onto her vanity and pulled on her riding boots.

Stevie didn't know if Blake would help her with her riding—he hadn't said anything that afternoon. He had just walked away, off the ranch, when they stopped work for dinner. But she wanted to see Jack Rabbit. And Buckaroo, and Satchmo, and even— She stopped herself. She just wanted to see her horses. She wanted to ride.

She wondered how far away she could get if she started riding now, and continued on and on. She sighed.

Outside, the sun was setting. Noticeably earlier now. Summer was ending. She sighed again.

She saw someone standing inside the corral. She thought at first it was Blake, waiting for her, after all, waiting to help her with her lead changes. But then she recognized

Travis. He had a bucket and a paintbrush, and was painting that side of the fence.

She walked up to the fence. He looked over the top of the fence at her. He had a smudge of paint on the side of his nose. Stevie resisted the urge to reach through the fence and wipe off the smudge with her thumb.

"What are you still doing here?" she asked, looking away, feeling her cheeks get warm and her thumb tingle at the thought of touching his face. "I thought you left."

"I did," Travis said. "But..." He focused on the fence again, touched it with the brush. "I didn't have anything else to do. So I figured I would finish this fence."

"Thanks." It sounded stupid as soon as she said it, but she meant it. She looked from Travis to the barn. Except for streaks on the wooden shingles and a scattering of spots on the dirt in the corral, her splatterings had been covered or removed. "I'm sorry," she added.

Travis looked at her. "It's just paint."

"Not that." She swallowed. "For all the yelling..."

"Don't worry about it."

Her gaze moved from the barn to the rest of the ranch. How good it looked. How close to her memories. And yet...

"It's just... it's just everything is so different now," she said. The admission came out before she could stop it. She didn't even know why she was telling Travis. What did he care? But she plowed on. "Everything. Ever since... Edwin died." She swallowed the grief that tried to well up, then went on. "Blake's leaving. Dad's... not here. Not really. Even when he's standing right in front of me. And... and we have to sell..." Her voice drifted off, choked by the tightness of her throat. She surprised herself. Had she already accepted that they would be leaving the ranch? Moving away? Had she known it all along and only just now admitted it to herself?

How had her summer of big plans come to this?

She looked at Travis. She—almost—wanted him to hold her again. Just hold her. The fence, though, wet paint still gleaming, stood between her and him. And something else. He met her eyes, but she didn't think he saw her.

"I'm sorry," he said.

Stevie stared at him. There he went again. Apologizing at the wrong moment. She shook her head. "It's not... you didn't do anything."

"I feel like I did."

Too late Stevie realized what he would say next. "No!"

But Travis, still not seeing her even as he looked right at her, didn't seem to hear her either. "If it wasn't for me, Edwin would still be here. It was my idea to go to the lake. My idea for us to come back so late. I should've known Mom would be—"

"Stop it!" Grief, memories of Edwin's face so pale and wax-like in his coffin, made her shout. "Do you want me to hate you?" She took a breath, tried to regain control. "I almost did, you know. Hate you."

Travis's eyes focused on her.

"At the funeral," she went on. "You were alive—and your Mom—and Edwin was dead."

"I wanted—" Travis's voice caught in his throat. He coughed. "I wanted to trade places with him. So bad."

"So did I," Stevie said, barely a whisper now. She had heard someone at the funeral say, *It's like he's sleeping.* She didn't remember who had said that. She only remembered the remark—and that she had wanted to strangle the speaker. Because if they had known Edwin at all, they would've known he never kept so still, even when sleeping. In the coffin he was just another boy. Not her brother with the beautiful eyes and the perfect smile, who teased her with calls of *Steevie Creevie the Pest.* The eyes and the smile and Steevie Creevie all were gone. It wasn't fair, she kept wanting to say. It wasn't Edwin. He wasn't sleeping. He was *gone.* It just wasn't fair. "I wanted to hate you."

"Do you?"

"No." She shook her head. "How stupid are you? I don't hate you. Because it wasn't your fault. It wasn't anyone's fault. Sometimes... sometimes... bad things happen. Sometimes," she added, "the people we love die." And sometimes they just leave, she didn't say.

He looked away. "I'm sorry," he said again.

"You're sorry?" Her grief changed into anger, and her voice got even louder than before. "Is that why you're here all the time? Is that why you kissed me? Because you felt *sorry* for me? Because you want me to *hate* you?"

Travis turned to face her again, opened his mouth to say something.

She cut him off by holding up her hand. No longer shouting, but with a growl in her voice, she said, "Don't *even* think you're going to say 'I'm sorry' again."

Travis closed his mouth.

Stevie gave him a short, curt nod. "Maybe you're not so stupid after all." She turned her head and pushed the tears out of her eyes. "I'm going to go see Jack Rabbit," she said. "Don't follow me," she added. "Not right now. I'll see you tomorrow."

Stevie sat on the fence of the southwest corral, where Dad had mended it, smiling—a tight, sad smile, but still a smile—at Jack Rabbit and the images of their first, winning race that he sent her. If the big horse noticed her sad, mad mood he didn't comment on it.

She had come out to ride, to practice with or without Blake's help. But she just sat there, remembering Edwin, remembering Mom, and remembering when the old, rotting fence of the southwest pasture that stretched away on either side of her had been new and strong and freshly painted.

Allison Keenan came two days later. Stevie wanted to hate the woman as she poked around the ranch, looking at the house and the barn, the corral and the pastures, chatting with Blake and taking notes in a blue spiral notebook. Peeking into their lives and their souls and writing inane notes like, "Barn freshly painted." But Stevie couldn't hate her. It wasn't Allison Keenan who had screwed up her life. Still, Stevie refused to meet the real estate agent.

She kept her distance, but she couldn't stay away. It was like watching someone through a dark, one-way mirror, watching them watch the movie of her life.

Here is where little Stevie learned to walk, the narrator would be saying. Here is where she fell down the porch steps, head first. And here is the corral where little Stevie rode her first horse. In that corner over there is where Stevie was thrown from her own horse, and kicked in the head just this past spring. Yes, it's true...

She saw Dad come out when Allison first arrived. Saw him shake her hand with a scowl, then leave Blake to take the real estate agent around the ranch.

Before she left, Allison had to go into the house and see Dad again. From the loft of the barn where she hid and watched, Stevie saw the woman come out of the house with a small bundle of paperwork. Then Allison took a "For Sale" sign out of the back of her big, blue SUV and pushed it into the ground at the end of the driveway.

As Stevie watched the SUV drive away a few minutes later, she wondered how much her life was being sold for.

Over the next week, Blake sometimes came out to watch her take Jack Rabbit around the barrels, but he seldom offered any suggestions or comments. Which was just fine with Stevie—and with Jack Rabbit. Any time Stevie thought about asking Blake for help, she would look up and see the "For Sale" sign, glaring and intensely bright in the hot August sun and casting a black shadow that seemed to stab into the ground.

And she remembered losing the last race.

She needed Blake to take her to the race at the end of the week. He had promised to take her, and she knew he still would. When Blake gave his word, he followed through—even if he was angry. But she didn't want his advice or his help.

She and Jack Rabbit ran the barrels at a controlled pace, alternating between a trot and a quick walk. They focused on taking the turns as tight as they could. They practiced *their* way.

Sometimes, Stevie found herself shifting her weight, using her legs the way Blake had tried to teach her. When that happened, she would do the turn again. *Their* way.

By Wednesday, both of Stevie's wrists ached, especially the left one, and her right ankle took to twinging on her at awkward moments. But in the saddle she forgot about the pain as she and Jack Rabbit ran as one creature, smooth and sharp. Jack Rabbit cooperated with her fully, even when she reined him in and kept him from going as fast as he could. So she gritted her teeth against the discomfort—and showed her teeth in a grim smile whenever Blake looked particularly upset about how she and Jack Rabbit took a turn.

Thursday, Travis noticed her wincing while she helped paint over the worst of the old fence boards. "Is your wrist bothering you again?"

Stevie gave him a smile that she hoped didn't look too much like a grimace. "I can handle it," she said. And to prove it, she picked up her bucket of paint with her left hand—ignoring the sharp, stabbing shocks that arced up her wrist and almost put tears in her eyes—and moved it to the next part of the fence.

Travis didn't look convinced, but he didn't mention it again. Later, she saw him watch her limp along, favoring her right ankle, and remembered waking up in the pasture after falling down, after that impossible run with the horses, opening her eyes to see his face.

Back on the first day of her summer. Only three days late. Back when she still thought she was going to have the best summer of her life.

She clenched her jaw and forced herself to walk normal. And forced herself not to think about Travis's eyes. Or his hands. Or his lips.

* * *

Jack Rabbit waited impatiently for her to groom him. This was the day of the race—*his* race—and she was being slow. Too slow. He stamped his foot and blew out.

"Sorry, boy." She held the curry brush in her right hand, stroking his back, while she pressed her left wrist against her chest. After her shower, in her room, she had noticed the wrist brace on her dresser where she had tossed it more than a month ago, on top of the still-unopened birthday card. Almost she had put the brace on. But she didn't want to answer the questions Blake would ask. And she wouldn't risk missing this race.

Jack Rabbit's race. The impression of possessive owner-ship came very clearly from the big horse.

"Our race," Stevie said.

Jack Rabbit snorted.

She smiled and shook her head. "Almost done."

Once again, as he had for the first race, Jack Rabbit let her lead him into the trailer without hesitation. He almost pushed her into the trailer in front of him.

He nudged her with his nose while she fastened the safety straps. Stevie saw an image of Jack Rabbit standing proud in the center of a cheering arena, flowers piled high around him, a winner. She laughed and kissed his nose.

"Ready?" Blake asked when she came out of the escape door of the trailer.

Stevie's smile faded. She nodded. Of course they were ready.

That was their only conversation of the morning.

Stevie stood beside Jack Rabbit, holding his rein and idly stroking his neck, waiting for their turn.

She felt detached. Though she could hear the sound of the crowded arena, and smell the scents of the horses and riders surrounding her, only the barest traces reached her. Jack Rabbit trembled with excitement beside her. She wished she could share his energy. This was their day.

This was their race. But ever since she had managed—just barely, as Jack Rabbit fidgeted and stamped, forcing her to hold the weight of the saddle, fighting not to drop it, trying not to cry out from the pain—to get Jack Rabbit ready, she had felt... separate.

Almost she had asked Blake to take her home—

Jack Rabbit snorted.

"Just almost," she said, patting his shoulder. Because there wasn't much left at home, anyway. Just Dad, probably still sleeping off the night before. And the "For Sale" sign. She squeezed her eyes shut and tried to concentrate. On riding. On winning. On anything else. "We're here to race, aren't we boy?"

Jack Rabbit nodded, then pulled on the reins. Of course he was here to race. Why else would he be here? He pointed his nose at the door.

"Soon," she said.

She felt alone. Except for Blake, she expected no one else she knew to be at the arena. Michelle and her family were away on vacation. Travis had asked her about the race the day before, but she didn't expect him to show up. A ninety minute drive was a long way to go for a sport that hardly interested him. Or to see a girl he had kissed only once.

Beside her, Jack Rabbit radiated excitement, his blood almost boiling. She could see, in her mind, the turns of the race, feel his need to run, his need to *win*.

She managed a smile for him.

Finally—or too soon—the door judge signaled her. She braced herself against the pain, and managed to suppress both the aches in her bones and the nervousness in her stomach as she climbed into the saddle. Jack Rabbit needed no urging to move forward and take the starting position. Stevie nodded to the man with the starting flag. They were as ready as they were going to be.

Jack Rabbit tensed, and so did Stevie, both of them waiting for the flag.

The flag streaked across her vision and made her blink.

Jack Rabbit didn't wait for her command. By the time she opened her eyes, the two of them were halfway to the first barrel, the rush of hot air pushing her hair back from her face. She tightened her grip on the reins, pushed her awareness into Jack Rabbit so that they ran as one, and prepared for the first turn.

To her surprise, she found she was directing the lead change for the turn the way Blake had wanted her to all summer. *The key to lead changes is in the hindquarters*, he had said over and over. *Not the weird way you're doing it.* After countless protests that she was doing it *her* way, hers and Jack Rabbit's, even after weeks of practicing her way in the evenings. And yet, Blake's way—*this is how Mom taught me to do it*, he had said—suddenly felt... right. *This* was how it was supposed to be done.

Her surprise and Jack Rabbit's frustration. He fought the lead change, stumbled through the turn, but didn't hit the barrel, and they were charging to the second barrel.

Jack Rabbit closed himself to her with a mental force that shocked her. An invisible door slammed her in the face and almost knocked her from the saddle.

The second barrel came at her while she still struggled to regain her grip with her hands and legs. The pain in her joints made it difficult, but she did it. She settled back to direct the turn.

Jack Rabbit ignored her. This time he took the turn *their* way, his and hers. No stumbling this time, and a pocket of less than three feet.

The stress on Jack Rabbit's left foreleg stabbed into Stevie's mind and made her gasp. The pain repeated, the hammer of the hoof striking the arena floor, driving the pain up his leg. Stevie felt the pain, but not in her body. Only in her mind. Jack Rabbit kept her separate, still refused to let her in, to let her direct him. Lightning shocks of indirect agony ground into her eyes. The pain didn't slow Jack Rabbit, though. He grabbed the bit in his teeth and plunged forward, dragging Stevie with him.

Stevie pulled on the reins and tried to push herself back into Jack Rabbit's mind. She had to. She could cushion the blows, take the damage into her own wrists and ankles, spare Jack Rabbit the pain and the injury.

But only if he would let her.

He refused.

The third turn was as perfect as the second. The pain she could feel but not share or relieve screamed in her mind and out of her mouth. She couldn't see through the haze of Jack Rabbit's agony, and she was powerless to stop him. She didn't know how he kept running. She couldn't see the arena, but she could see that every stride hit Jack Rabbit harder and harder, every jolt threatening to tear him apart.

Yet he still ran.

He was going to win. That was all that mattered to him. A little pain—only enough to nearly kill Stevie—wasn't going to stop Jack Rabbit. And neither was Stevie. She was just a weight he had to carry.

Jack Rabbit's leg held together until they had crossed the finish line. Then, as if watching it happen in slow motion, with the harsh accuracy and detail of an x-ray, Stevie saw the bones and sinews, muscles and tendons, unravel. She screamed again.

Jack Rabbit crumpled forward, his left foreleg breaking in a drawn out tattoo of wet snaps and cracks.

Jack Rabbit screamed.

For all that she had lived around horses her entire life, Stevie had never heard a horse scream. The sound ripped through her soul and burned into her mind and she knew she would never forget it.

Jack Rabbit's left shoulder hit the arena floor. His hind-quarters came up, pushing Stevie up as well.

Stevie thought she might be thrown clear, but then felt her boots caught in the stirrups, felt Jack Rabbit's weight pressing down on her left leg, saw the ground rushing at her, and everything went black.

Chapter 11
Waking Up

STEVIE CAME TO hearing Jack Rabbit's continued scream and the sounds of the arena and men shouting. Rough hands were pulling her away from the warm, thrashing bulk of Jack Rabbit. Beyond a veil of her own shock and grogginess, she knew Jack Rabbit was in agony. She tried to fight the hands, tried to crawl back to be with Jack Rabbit.

I need to go to him, she tried to say. *Jack Rabbit needs me. I can help him.* But all she managed to do was cough out a gob of dirt and gravel and blood.

The hands dragging her back, away from Jack Rabbit, loosened their grip. Stevie tried to sit up, but the hands returned. They held her down. The lights of the arena hovered far above her, more of them than she remembered. And faces swam around her. And still Jack Rabbit's screams.

The truth of his injury slammed into Stevie. She had seen—felt!—what had happened to his leg. She wondered if he would ever be able to race again. She wondered if she would. But she could help him. She would break her own arm to help him. Both of her arms if she had to. It couldn't be too late. She had to be able to help him. She tried to get up again.

"Stay still, Stevie. Stay still. The doctor's coming."

The voice, barely audible over the cacophony, sounded like Dad, and the unexpectedness of it penetrated Stevie's awareness. She tried to focus on the face of the man that held her shoulders. Maybe Dad. Her eyes wouldn't cooperate. Or Blake. Probably not Travis. She looked around for Edwin but didn't see him. Or would've looked around had not hands suddenly clamped on her head to keep her from moving. She wondered where Mom was.

She felt something sharp jab her, except it wasn't her. It was Jack Rabbit. A new layer of haze spread across her mind, separating her from Jack Rabbit still more. The horse's screams subsided and his thrashing stopped. His mind drifted further away from hers.

Let me go, she tried to say. All that came out was another cough. *He needs ...*

Fingers pushed into her mouth, pressed her tongue down, fished out dirt. And maybe one of her teeth. She hoped it was just a bit of gravel.

He needs me, she tried to say. Breathing was easier now, but she had no more luck saying the words than in making the hands let her go. She reached for Jack Rabbit, with her left hand, with her heart, but couldn't get any closer. She couldn't touch him. And he was farther and farther away, through thicker and thicker layers of gauze.

Crying, sobbing, coughing, still trying to get free of the hands and move to Jack Rabbit, Stevie lost consciousness once again.

She woke up in a room she didn't recognize. White ceiling, pale walls, bright lights. And Blake, of course.

And Dad.

She tried to sit up. The room tilted and her stomach threatened to leave her completely and there were suddenly two Dad's and two Blake's, all four of them looking concerned and reaching for her. She laid back against the pillow. Not her pillow in not her bed in not her room.

"Stay still, Stevie," Blake said, his voice echoing oddly in her head. "The doctor said you shouldn't try to sit up. Not yet. You had a concussion."

Stevie forced her eyes to focus on Blake despite the pounding in her head. He looked awful. His hair stuck out in all directions, as if he'd been running his hands through it. And his eyes showed the signs that he had been crying.

"It's OK," she said, wanting to comfort him. "I survived—"

Then the pounding in her head hit her between the eyes and she heard again Jack Rabbit's scream. She clenched her eyes closed against the suddenly too bright light and the remembered pain.

When she opened her eyes again, both Blake and Dad stood over her, each of them holding one of her hands. Dad with his other hand on her head, fingers lightly stroking her hair.

She didn't look at Dad. "Jack—Jack Rabbit?" she asked Blake. She didn't want to ask Dad. If she looked at Dad she would know. She wouldn't have to ask. And she had to be able to ask. "Will he be—can he race?"

Blake met her eyes, then looked away. "We don't know."

"Don't know what?" Stevie asked, but Blake just shook his head.

Finally Stevie looked at Dad. He met her eyes, didn't look away. "His—Jack Rabbit's leg—is broken," he said. "Very badly broken."

Stevie tried to read Dad's face. But all she could see was his concern for her. She could feel it through his fingertips on her face. As if she was important. As if she was the most important thing in the world. Had he been at the race? Like she remembered? She almost asked. But there was another question she had to ask first. "Will Jack Rabbit be able to race again?"

"I don't know, Stevie," Dad said.

But Stevie knew. She had felt the break happen. The tears came and she didn't even try to stop them. It was her fault. She had let Jack Rabbit down. All he had ever wanted was to race, and now he wouldn't be able to. Because of her. "Will he..." The lights flared again, turning her tears into brilliant stars, and the room spun. Only Dad's hand on her forehead seemed to anchor her, and Dad and Blake holding her hands. She felt the darkness coming for her. She fought it off, forced the words out of her mouth. "Will he be able to—to race again?"

Dad shook his head. "I don't know, Stevie," he said again. "We just don't know. Doc Siemers has him at his place. He says the break can be healed..." His voice became faint as Stevie felt herself sink into darkness. Dad's words about tendons and splints and knitting bones faded into a buzz until it stopped altogether. Then she thought she heard him say one more thing. "Stevie, I'm sorry." She could barely hear him. She didn't know if he was really talking, or if she were already dreaming. "I'm..." An echo, or a pause, Stevie couldn't be sure. Then the sound of Dad's voice breaking. "I'm so sorry."

The sound of Dad crying nearly brought her back. He needed her, and she wanted to comfort him. But the darkness wouldn't let her go.

The sunlight coming in her window—poking her in the eye—woke Stevie. Squinting to reduce the glare, she guessed—and her alarm clock confirmed—that it was about nine in the morning.

She had slept in. Neither Dad nor Blake had come up to wake her. But one of them had—thoughtfully—left her blinds open so the sun would do the job.

She tried to sit up, so she could at least get up and shut the blinds on the too, too bright sunlight, but the throbbing in her head made her lie back down, her hands holding her head together, fingers covering her clenched eyes. Questions made her mind hurt as much as her head. Was it Sunday? Why did her head hurt? Why was she still in bed if it wasn't Sunday? Why did she ache all over?

When did she have to go back to school? Where was Jack Rabbit?

The sound of a truck maneuvering, crunching over the gravel of the driveway in front of the house, made it through the haze, the hurt, and her hands. Then the sound of men's voices, greeting each other. The sound of a ramp falling and striking the gravel. More talking.

So it probably wasn't Sunday.

Stevie dared to take her fingers off her eyes, then—gingerly—took her hands from the sides of her head. Her eyes blinked but she could see again. And her head seemed to stay together.

Her eyes focused on the back of her left hand and the small bandages and the scabbed-over abrasions on her knuckles.

The first thing she remembered was Jack Rabbit kicking her in the head.

Her fingers found the scar on her lip and for the first time in her life really understood *deja vu*. Because spring break was *months* ago—even if she couldn't remember what day it was *now*. It was spring break when she had been in the hospital, and then spent the rest of her week in her own room, waking up late in the morning, hearing the sounds of the Buckbee Ranch through her window, wishing she could tell Jack Rabbit that she understood, that it wasn't his fault. Wishing Dad and Blake would stop hovering over her. Wishing they would take her plans for the summer seriously. And wishing that Dad wouldn't make himself a drink every time he came into the house to check on her.

All of that was long ago. She had ridden Jack Rabbit since then—

She wanted to remember what day it was. But she couldn't. Saturday? Tuesday? Easter?

Not that it mattered. Another question pushed that one from her mind: *Where is Jack Rabbit?*

She managed to sit up and swing her legs off the bed. She needed to find Jack Rabbit. He needed her. She couldn't remember *why*, but the need was enough. She had to go to him.

Dad had been so upset when Jack Rabbit kicked her. He had threatened to sell Jack Rabbit. He and Stevie had argued over and over.

But that was months ago. Dad had relented, and she and Jack Rabbit had trained, and even raced—

Had they won? Her eyes found the gold-plated statue of a horse and rider on her shelf. A trophy. Her trophy. Hers and Jack Rabbit's.

Where was Jack Rabbit?

She stood up, and waited for the room to slow down, then stop. From the north window, the one that wasn't trying to blind her, she heard the nicker of a horse. Her first thought was *Jack Rabbit!*, but then she recognized Satchmo, from the tenor of his voice and from the image that appeared in her mind.

A truck, and Satchmo. Where was Satchmo going?

At the window, leaning against the sill, looking down through the blinds, she saw Stan Harrison's big Ford truck, with a short horse trailer hitched up. The ramp to the trailer was down and she saw Blake—no, not Blake; Dad; of course Dad; why did that seem so unusual?—leading Satchmo into the trailer.

Satchmo paused, pulling back against the lead, to look up at her and meet her eyes.

In her mind Stevie saw Jack Rabbit standing in the pasture, beautiful and proud. And then she saw Jack Rabbit galloping along the fence, and Jack Rabbit prancing and telling the story of how he won his first race. A hint of sadness tinged the images, and regret. And genuine dislike. Yet she knew that Satchmo was offering his best wishes. And his farewells.

A man's voice in her head, low and gravelly. *Good-bye, Stevie.*

Then Satchmo yielded to Dad's lead and walked into the trailer.

Stevie tried to reply, but she couldn't find her voice, as she remembered everything.

She winced at the restored memory of the shared pain of Jack Rabbit's leg failing and breaking. And felt new tears at the guilt. She should have been able to help him, to take the pain and the injury on herself.

It's not your fault. Satchmo's voice in her head was faint as he told her the same thing Dad had said to her over and over the past days. In the hospital, on the way home, and last night before he kissed her and turned off the light.

Stevie didn't believe Satchmo either. Jack Rabbit, stabled at Doc Siemers for at least another week, should be able to carry riders again. But his racing days were almost certainly over. Three races, two wins, and his—and her—career of racing was over. And it was all her fault.

She felt Satchmo snort in reply, but the horse said nothing more.

Stevie watched Dad and Stan Harrison put up the ramp and fasten it in place, then shake hands. "Good-bye," she finally managed to whisper as Satchmo drove away with his owner to find a new stable.

After her shower, and a good look at the yellow bruise on her forehead—this bruise didn't seem to be healing as fast as the ones earlier in the summer—Stevie pulled on a pair of jeans and a t-shirt, stomped her feet into her work boots, and went downstairs. She clutched the handrail, and tried to force the stairs not to seem quite so *steep*.

She still didn't know what day it was. She tried to puzzle it out as she navigated the stairs. The race had been Saturday. At least one of the days in the hospital had been a Tuesday. Had that been yesterday? Or the day before?

Dad came in the front door as she finally reached the bottom of the stairs. Surprise showed on his face when he saw her. And another emotion that Stevie wasn't sure about, a darkness behind his eyes. But he wasn't angry.

"You shouldn't be up, honey," Dad said. "I was about to go up and look in on you."

Stevie held onto the banister for support, used it to stand up straight. "I need to see Jack Rabbit," she said.

She expected Dad to argue with her, but he only nodded and moved to help her. He put his arm around her waist and took most of her weight. "Did you want to eat breakfast first?"

The foyer shifted around her, from the lingering effects of the concussion or Dad's easy acquiescence or hunger or... she didn't know. But suddenly breakfast sounded like a good idea. "Breakfast first," she said.

Dad led her to the kitchen and helped her sit at the table. She watched, unsure what she was seeing, as Dad made her breakfast of scrambled eggs and toast. She tried to remember the last time Dad had made her breakfast. Before Edwin died, certainly. Had it been so long ago? How could one year stretch so far back into the past?

"How long has," she started, then stopped. She put her thoughts and her words in order. "What day is it?"

Dad paused in pushing the eggs around in the frying pan. To Stevie, it looked like he considered several options before finally saying, "Thursday."

Nearly a week lost. And her last race of the summer was next week—

Except she had already raced her last race. So she cut that thought off.

After he put the plate down in front of her, Dad poured himself a cup of coffee and sat. He watched her as she ate. It seemed like a lot of food when she started, but she ate it all.

"Where's Blake?" she asked between bites.

"He and Travis are working on the front gate." There might have been a slight pause before Travis's name, but Stevie couldn't be sure. "Painting it," he added.

She still expected Dad to argue with her, to tell her that she should wait before going to see Jack Rabbit. And she was ready to tell him that she had to go. That it was like getting back on the horse that threw you. But he said nothing else.

Stevie looked at her empty plate and considered asking for more. Then decided not to risk it. She didn't want to get sick and give Dad an excuse not to take her to Doc Siemers. So she stood and—after a second or so—took her plate and fork to the sink. She noticed the empty bottle of scotch whiskey in the trash can by the sink.

She sighed, and turned to Dad. "Do you...do I need to ask Blake to take me?"

"No." He finished his coffee, placing the empty cup down on the table. "I'll take you. You ready?"

She nodded. With breakfast strengthening her, Stevie thought she could have walked down the front steps by herself, but Dad seemed to want to help her. So she let him.

"I'm not a baby," she said as he all but lifted her into the passenger seat of his truck. Because Blake—or worse, Travis—might be watching.

He smiled, then surprised her for the third time that morning by leaning over and kissing her on the forehead. Like he had last night, tucking her into bed for the first time since she was six. "You'll always be my Baby Girl." His breath smelled of coffee.

Stevie couldn't think of anything to say. They were already in gear, moving slowly down the long driveway, before Stevie realized that there had not been even a hint of scotch on his breath. Not last night. Not now.

Dad pulled up just before the gate, and rolled down his window. Blake and Travis were painting the big metal gate. Blake was on a tall ladder—only his waist and legs were visible this close—while Travis worked on the lower sections. Both had their shirts off. The wet white paint— and the sweat on their bare shoulders—gleamed in the late morning sunshine.

Travis stood up and looked past Dad to Stevie. Stevie started to wave, but the intensity of his look—and his bare torso—made her look away before she turned green and sank into the bottom of the truck cab. So instead of looking at Travis she looked up at the freshly painted metal letters that announced the Buckbee Horse Ranch, backward from this side of the gate. She hoped her suddenly pounding heart couldn't be heard all the way into town.

"We're headed over to Doc Siemers," Dad told Blake, leaning out the window and looking up. "Need anything?"

"No," Blake said. "We're good."

"We'll be back in a bit."

Stevie was still looking up at the sign as Dad's window whirred back up.

"I think Travis expected at least a wave or something," Dad said.

She could hear the amusement in his voice, but refused to look at him. She started to smile an embarrassed smile, but her eyes, coming down as Dad put the truck into gear and started forward again, landed on the "For Sale" sign. A "Contract Pending" banner had been added to the top of the sign. She didn't remember seeing that last night, but it had been dark. Her smile died as Dad turned onto the county road. With her need to see Jack Rabbit, and with the surprises Dad kept springing on her this morning, she had forgotten.

Her summer was ending.

Dr. Siemers gave his prognosis as he led them into the large barn behind his office. The vet's barn smelled like almost every other barn Stevie had been in: manure, musk, and hay. But there was also a chemical undertone of cleaners and medicine that put her on edge.

"Jack Rabbit's a young horse," Dr. Siemers was saying, "so he should be as good as new in ten to twelve months."

Stevie heard him but paid no attention. She looked at Jack Rabbit. He hung suspended from a harness in a wide stall, his head to the center of the barn, his left foreleg encased from the shoulder to the ground in a fiberglass cast. His head hung low. In the fluorescent lighting of the barn, his coat seemed flat and muddy. She could feel the pain in his leg, and the pressure of the bandages and the cast, and the dullness of the painkillers in his muscles and blood.

"I'm keeping him here for a few more days, Dr. Siemers went on, "but he should be able to go home soon, once I'm certain he's used to the cast and that leg is taking at least most of its share of his weight..."

Jack Rabbit's ears perked as they came closer and he looked up. He met Stevie's eyes with one of his, but offered her no mental images.

"I'm sorry, boy," she said, her voice a tight whisper. Neither Dad nor Dr. Siemers seemed to notice she said anything.

Jack Rabbit's right ear twitched, but he still didn't respond. He already knew she was sorry. Sorry didn't make the pain go away. Sorry wouldn't fix his leg.

"I would have—" she started to say, but his silent stare cut her off. She wanted to tell him that she would have gladly broken her arm to save his, but he wasn't listening.

He just looked at her, then looked away.

Stevie felt her heart break inside her. He blamed her. She understood, though. She blamed herself. She hung back and watched as Dr. Siemers and Dad stood next to Jack Rabbit, talking. Dr. Siemers's left hand idly stroked Jack Rabbit's nose as he talked and she wished it was her hand. She wished she could be the one to comfort Jack Rabbit. She wished she could just touch him.

"Did you hear that, Stevie?" Dad asked.

Stevie looked at Dad. "What?"

"Haven't you been listening? Doc Siemers's been saying that you and Jack Rabbit should be able to race again next summer."

Race again. Next summer. The words hit her but didn't penetrate. They seemed impossible. Dr. Siemers smiled when she looked at him for confirmation.

"Absolutely," he said. "No guarantees, of course, but if we can keep him healthy and keep the bones knitting properly—and if someone can teach both horse and rider how to take those barrels in a less headlong, suicidal manner—then I don't see why you couldn't be racing again next summer."

Dr. Siemers kept talking, but Stevie was no longer listening to him. She rushed up to Jack Rabbit and threw her arms around his neck and hugged him tight.

"Hey, hey," Dr. Siemers said, interrupting himself. "That leg's not healed yet. You need to go easy."

Stevie ignored the man and ignored the sudden pain that danced up and down her left arm. She felt only the surge from touching Jack Rabbit again, his stiff coat hairs against the bare skin of her arms and her fingers in his mane, his scent in her nostrils. "Did you hear that, boy? We're going to race again. We're going to race again."

Jack Rabbit kept his head up, refusing to nuzzle her, still refusing to talk to her. Still blaming her.

After a long minute of mixed joy and sadness and guilt and the embarrassment and loneliness of hugging someone who won't return the embrace, Stevie let go and backed up. She kept trying to meet Jack Rabbit's eye. She tried not to cry.

She waited for Dad and Dr. Siemers to finish some of the paperwork required by the insurance company, never taking her eyes off Jack Rabbit. But he wouldn't look at her.

Blake was finishing the front gate alone when Stevie and Dad returned from the vet. Dad hadn't said anything on the way home. But neither had she.

After they parked in front of the house, Stevie walked back down the driveway toward the gate. The driveway looked much different now than it had ten weeks ago. New gravel had been spread, and the grass along the both sides, next to the freshly painted wooden fences, had been mowed. The entire ranch looked as good as new. Or at least as good as Stevie could remember seeing it.

"Looking for Travis?" Blake asked when she got close enough.

"No!" Stevie said, because she wasn't, then asked, "Where did he go?"

Blake shrugged, then bent over and picked up his shirt off the grass by the fence. "Said he had to go do something." He wiped his face with the shirt and draped it around his neck.

Stevie climbed up to the top rail of the fence and sat down facing Blake. She had thought about Blake on the drive home, and when she saw him working alone, she had decided she needed to talk to him. Now, though, she pointed to the for sale sign. "I go into a coma, and you sell the ranch. Just like that." It came out harsher than she intended. She gave a weak smile to soften it. She wasn't here to fight.

"Yeah," Blake said, leaning against the fence beside her. "It's like you were in the way, or something. And then you weren't."

Stevie decided she was too weak to properly punch him, so she settled for sticking out her tongue.

"Allison called Monday afternoon," Blake went on. "Dad refused to leave you, so I was here Tuesday morning for the inspection. Dad signed the contract Tuesday night. He still hasn't met the buyers."

"Anyone we know?"

"No. A couple out of Dallas."

"So," Stevie said, and then stopped. She sighed. "It's over?"

Blake nodded. "I guess so."

Stevie stared at nothing, trying not to think about spending another year in Tulsa—this time with no home to come back to.

After a moment, Blake asked, "Do you remember what today is?" His voice had an unfamiliar tenor to it.

"Thursday," Stevie said. She wondered when Uncle Rick and Aunt Mary would be down to pick her up and take her away again.

"It's August 9th."

Stevie gripped the top of the fence with both hands to steady herself against the new disorientation that threatened her balance. All thoughts of Tulsa and Uncle Rick and Aunt Mary receded. In their place exploded memories of Edwin, him laughing and riding and, finally, lying in his coffin, his eyes closed and his hair so unnaturally still. She remembered him grabbing a towel, a ball cap, and a Frisbee, running out of the house with Travis, heading to the lake. Had that only been a year ago? The last time she saw him? "I... I didn't know," she managed to whisper.

"I hadn't thought of it at all," Blake said, his voice low, making Stevie look at him. "Until Saturday, when I saw you..." He swallowed, making his Adam's apple go up and down. "When I saw you plough face first into the dirt with a horse on top of you. For an instant—for what seemed like one second that stretched out forever—I thought, 'Oh my god. I'm going to lose her too.' I saw the same thought in Dad's face when he got to the hospital." He stopped, the muscles of his jaw clenched. After a few seconds, his face relaxed and he looked at her, meeting her eyes. "Thanks for not dying," he said.

Feeling stupid—and thinking how stupid it was that Blake just wouldn't *cry*, or at least give her a hug when he said things like that—Stevie just nodded in reply.

Blake pushed off the fence, standing up straight again, and started to walk away.

"Wait."

Blake stopped and turned to face her again.

"I just... I just wanted to say that I don't think you're... you're running away. That's what I came over to say. I don't understand why you want to go so far away..." Thoughts of Edwin and Mom and Blake's arguments with Dad pushed into her mind. "Or maybe I do," she went on. "But only so long as you come back. You have to come back."

He came back to her then and hugged her, pressing her face into his damp shirt. He smelled of sweat and paint and his back was sticky, but she hugged him anyway.

"I'm going to miss you," she said.

He released her. "I'm going to miss you too," he said. "Some."

"Sweaty jerk," she said, and pushed him, hard. But the effect was lost when she had to grab his arms to keep from falling off the fence.

The remaining horses were in the northeast pasture, standing in small groups under the limited shade. They nickered and tossed their heads when Stevie came through the gate, but they didn't move out into the hot sunshine.

She held onto the gate for a few seconds after closing it behind her. She was tired. Exhausted even. More than she thought she should be so early in the afternoon. But she wasn't going to go back to the house. Not yet. Dad would probably insist she stay in the rest of the day as soon as she did. And she needed to be with her horses.

She had already missed Satchmo. And quite a few others, she saw. She counted only sixteen horses in the pasture. At least she had been able to say good-bye to Satchmo, if only briefly.

She moved to the closest group of five horses, and noticed that they were all stabled horses. None of the Buckbee horses were in the group. Still, they opened up to her when she walked among them. She stroked their noses and hugged their necks. She didn't have any treats, but the horses didn't seem to mind. The images that barraged her from all sides like the nuzzles and nudges were friendly and supportive. They had no wish to leave, but they understood.

Stevie felt better as she talked to them and touched them, stronger even. She had half expected them to shun her, to blame her. But all of them were happy to see her.

They were glad to see her walking and recovering. None of them seemed to explicitly blame Jack Rabbit for what had happened, but there was something of that nature within their best wishes for Jack Rabbit. And all of them seemed to bump and nudge her closer to Rain.

Buckaroo came up to her, stepping out of the shade to meet her. He nudged her with his head, and in her mind she saw an image of herself riding him around the barrels.

"Not today, boy. But soon. Soon."

Buckaroo nickered in happy anticipation. Like the rest, though, he sensed she had more on her mind, and he gestured with his head. Toward Rain.

Rain waited for her in the deepest part of the shade. Stevie hesitated, unsure, a few yards away.

"I'm sorry," she said. It didn't seem like enough. Just two words could hardly wipe out almost a whole summer's worth of deliberate snubbing, but it was all she could think of to say. "Jack Rabbit... he's hurt... the vet says he'll—we'll—race again, but he won't talk to me." The words, once started, came out in a rush. "He won't even look at me. I wanted to help him... I *tried* to help him, but he blocked me out. Like I blocked you... and I'm sorry. I'm so sorry. But it's all gone. Mom's gone, Edwin's gone. The ranch is being sold, Blake is going and Dad..." She looked at the ground in front of her feet, then closed her eyes to wipe away the tears. "What am I going to do?"

Rain's cheek brushed against Stevie's as the horse stepped close and rested her head on Stevie's shoulder. Stevie wrapped her arms around Rain's neck and pushed her face into the warmth of the mare's coat.

Rain didn't speak, but images opened in Stevie's mind. A little girl sitting in the corner of a horse stall, knees pulled up to her chin, long hair around her face, eyes red and puffy from crying, straw all over her clothes and in her hair. The little girl's face up close. The sensation of blowing, one quick puff, to push the disheveled hair out of the girl's eyes, followed by the scent of the little girl, of straw and salty tears and sweat and lingering shampoo and soap—and just a hint of her mother's perfume.

The smell of the perfume opened long-forgotten memories of her own behind Stevie's eyes and she saw Mom, tall and slender and beautiful in her riding boots and dark blue jeans and red-and-blue cowboy shirt, bending down to pick up Stevie and hug her close while Stevie hugged her about the neck and breathed in that wonderful smell. Then Mom laughed and kissed her on the mouth and wrinkled her nose and put her down and walked away.

And she saw Mom riding Rain, racing the barrels, pocketing the barrels with precision, cornering as if they were a single, beautiful creature. The view shifted and Stevie saw the race with Rain, watching the ground race and the barrels loom large, feeling Mom on her back, detecting the subtle shifts in leg muscles and position and feet in the stirrups, carrying them both around and through the turns and to the finish line. Like the story of the first race that Jack Rabbit would tell, but much smoother and with a grace that took Stevie's breath away.

Then she saw Mom running with the horses in the bright, hot sunshine of early summer, hair streaming behind her like the mane of a new, beautiful kind of horse—

Rain's amused snort startled her, and she realized she wasn't seeing Mom. She was seeing herself.

Finally, she remembered sitting in Rain's stall and crying the day that Dad told her Mom wasn't coming home. She had never been sure before that she hadn't dreamed that, only wished it had happened. She had run outside, away from Dad and his sad, defeated face and his sad eyes that wouldn't cry, and found herself in a dark corner of the barn. Needing someone, anyone, she had broken the rules Mom and Dad had both told her over and over, and went into Rain's stall by herself. Rain had been lying down, but stood as Stevie opened the stall and came in.

Stevie's memory and Rain's blended together then, and she felt both her own sadness and that of Rain, as both of them came to grips with being left by the most important person in their lives. Rain laid down again, making a space for the little girl Stevie and the little girl Stevie curled up beside her Mom's horse and the two of them grieved. Dad had found them like that, girl and horse. Stevie had no memory of him picking her up, gently, trying not to wake the little girl or disturb the horse. Of him putting her head on his shoulder, her long legs trailing down in front of him as he walked. Or of her putting her arms around his neck and pushing her face into his neck, never even opening her eyes.

Even with her eyes closed, with her arms still around Rain's neck, Stevie knew that Travis was walking toward her. The thoughts of the other horses in the pasture came to her. At first the thoughts had been vague. *A man is coming.* And she had thought maybe Dad or Blake had come to find her. Then the images of Travis had come, accompanied by his particular scent of sweat and boy musk, though overlaid with a fading scent of tears, along with a few flickering memories of a younger Travis and Edwin playing and riding and being boys.

Perhaps because she had been so sad all day, these memories of Edwin didn't make her cry. She almost smiled as she watched Edwin walking the top beam of the fence around the northeast pasture like a high-wire artist, arms extended, flailing as he lost his balance. Dad had yelled at all of them over the years that they shouldn't walk on the fences like that. It loosened the boards and they could spook the horses. The memories became a moving history. Edwin as a little boy, growing up to become a young man. Sometimes Blake was in the memories, and sometimes Stevie. Sometimes Dad. A few times—very few—they were all of them there, Dad, Blake, Edwin and Stevie, working the horses or doing chores together.

She smiled as she experienced the memories, but there were new tears when she finally opened her eyes and turned her head to see Travis. She felt his sadness, an emotional echo of her own feelings, visible in his eyes and the line of his mouth, and picked up and reflected from the horses. She seemed to see him, smell him, feel him from a dozen different vantages. The view of an individual by a herd. She tightened her grip on Rain to anchor herself.

Travis stopped a few steps away from her and Rain. He had showered—she could smell it, or the horses could, it was getting hard to tell the difference—and changed into fresh blue jeans and a pullover shirt with a collar. His boots had been wiped clean too. He looked like—and the memory made Stevie's throat hurt—he looked the way he had at Edwin's funeral.

"All dressed up," Stevie managed to say.

His lips moved into a tight smile, and his eyes averted as he nodded. He met her eyes, then looked away again. "You look good," he said. "I mean, it's good to see you. Up and around. And you always..." He paused and swallowed. "You always look so... pretty... when you're with your horses."

Stevie thought she saw his cheeks flush, then got distracted by the warmth of her own face and had to look away.

After a few seconds, Travis said, "Your Dad sent me to find you."

"Dad?" Stevie said, looking at him again. Of all the things she expected him to say—that one had never occurred to her. She couldn't remember Dad saying anything to Travis all summer.

He nodded. "I asked if it was alright if I came with you today. He said it was OK."

"Where are we going...?" she started to ask, then she knew. Of course. She turned her face away and pushed it against Rain, squeezing the horse's thick neck even tighter than before. Rain gave a light nicker and returned the hug as best she could. After a minute, Stevie let go and kissed Rain on the nose. Travis still stood there when she turned around.

She looked him up and down again. "Are you sure Edwin will recognize you?" she asked, trying to be funny. She wished she hadn't as soon as she saw his expression. He started to turn away from her, but she stepped up and put a hand on his arm, stopping him. "I'm sure he will."

They didn't say anything else as they walked across the pasture, through the corral, to the house. Dad's truck was there, but there was no sign of him or Blake, so Stevie went inside.

The glass door shut behind her, leaving her alone in the foyer. She looked over her shoulder and saw Travis sit on the porch swing.

"Did you find her?" Dad asked, his voice coming from his office.

"It's me." Stevie stood where she was, not wanting to see Dad at his desk, pouring himself a drink, or taking a drink. Not today.

"Are you OK?" The sound of a chair being pushed back followed the question, and Dad appeared in the arched doorway. He still wore his jeans and work boots from earlier, but he had changed his shirt. And shaved. "Are you OK?" he asked again, coming to her. He put his hands on her shoulders. "I meant to tell you earlier, but I didn't want you to think you had to go."

Stevie looked up at him. "Of course I have to go."

Dad let out a breath, not quite a sigh, then nodded.

The sadness in his eyes made Stevie hug him, even tighter than she had hugged Rain. She wondered how hard she would have to squeeze to make him cry.

Stevie hadn't been to Edwin's grave since the funeral service. She had only the vaguest recollection of where his plot was. When she tried to think of it, all she could remember was flowers and the awful click-click-click sound of the casket being lowered into the ground.

She stepped out of the truck, into the hot August sunshine and looked at the green field with its low trees and aging headstones and statues. Nothing looked familiar. She felt lost.

Dad, Blake and Travis, though, moved as one, not talking as they walked along the path and stepped between plots. Stevie followed them, walking near Blake, reading each headstone they came to, looking for Edwin's name, wondering how many times Dad and Blake had come here. And wondering why she had never thought to come. How could she have not come? Even once? In a whole year? His birthday had been while she was in Tulsa, but that hardly seemed an excuse. What kind of sister was she?

Finally Dad stopped and bent down on one knee and wiped dust and grass clippings from a small, rectangular headstone that lay flat against the ground. Stevie read the name as Dad's fingers traced the carved letters, "Edwin James Buckbee, November 14, 1991 - August 9, 2006". The grass of his plot looked as perfect as any lawn, as if it had never been disturbed to bury her brother.

In January, on her birthday, Stevie realized she would be as old as Edwin.

Blake put a hand on her shoulder as she started crying.

"I'm sorry."

Travis's words reached her and she opened her eyes to tell him to stop saying that. But Travis wasn't talking to her, wasn't even facing her. Instead, he looked up at Dad— except he wasn't looking up that much. Not anymore. The two of them stood almost eye to eye.

Stevie saw complicated emotions race across Dad's face. His eyes locked with Travis's. His hands at his sides twitched, then moved slowly, toward Travis, and gripped Travis's shoulders. Stevie looked at Blake beside her, hoping he would intervene. Blake's eyes flicked to meet hers then looked back to Dad and Travis.

So suddenly that Stevie almost cried out, Dad pulled Travis to his chest and wrapped his arms around the boy, holding him tight. "Me too," Dad said. He opened his mouth as if to say something more, then paused, and said it again, "Me too."

And for the first time in her life Stevie saw Dad cry.

Chapter 12
The Last Race of the Summer

Up in the saddle, Stevie clenched the reins and looked out at the bright arena. The floor was covered with dirt churned by hundreds of hooves, and the three barrels were arranged and waiting for her. She listened to the sounds of the crowd and the blare of the announcer, hearing none of the words, only the noise. She smelled horses and sweat and manure. Her stomach had climbed up into her chest and she wanted to throw up. The last time she had felt this nervous had been her first race of the summer. She had managed to not throw up then, she told herself. She would not throw up now.

"You ready?" Dad asked.

Stevie nodded. She hoped she didn't look as sick as she felt. Sick or not, though, she was ready.

"Barrel racing is won in the turns," Dad said.

Stevie only nodded in response. She didn't trust her voice. Besides, she knew that barrel racing was won in the turns. Because how many times had he said that in the last ten minutes? In the last week? She wasn't sure she could count that high. Dad said it even more than Blake ever did.

She thought—no, she *knew*—she had seen Rita Kaltenbach in the stands. Three thousand people she didn't know, and she sees the one woman most likely to be displeased with her. Then she found herself looking for Travis. Except he had told her he couldn't make it and she wished he could make it anyway. And that made her feel even more like she would throw up.

Stevie could feel the other horses in the arena. Some of them had nickered at Rain and sent her images of memories. A few Stevie thought she recognized from her other races that summer. She didn't know their names, but she knew the feel of their minds. She didn't open herself to them, though, beyond acknowledging their greetings. She focused on Rain and the race ahead of them.

Rain tried to sooth her, but she could feel Rain's own excitement through the muscles of her legs, and in the back of her mind. The old mare trembled with anticipation. This was Rain's first race in more than seven years. Horse and girl told themselves and each other that they were ready, rehearsing the route, taking the turns, already racing together in their shared minds.

Through Rain's memories, Stevie saw a younger version of Dad standing beside her, looking so much like Blake she missed her brother even more. Blake had left for Stillwater two weeks ago. He had called to say he would be here today, but he might be late. She wondered if he had arrived yet.

In Rain's memories she also saw a younger version of Rita Kaltenbach, standing where Dad was standing now. Stevie found herself wondering if she really did look like Mom from up there in the stands. And she surprised herself by not immediately getting angry at the thought. Instead she wished Mom were there, and could see her race. She might even forgive Mom for everything else in the last seven years, if only—

Stevie blinked to clear tears out of her eyes, and pushed thoughts of Mom out of her mind. She thought of Blake again. She had drawn an early position in the event. She hoped Blake wasn't so late he missed her race. Hopefully Blake had left Shannon at OSU—or wherever he left her. That girl would make him even later than he usually was.

The same day Blake left—with Shannon, unfortunately—to drive up to Stillwater and Oklahoma State University, Stevie and Dad, father and daughter, had been sitting on the front porch, enjoying the Sunday sunset over the Buckbee Ranch for one of the last times they ever would. Dad had asked Stevie if she felt up to one more race of the summer. "Two weeks isn't much time to get used to a whole new horse—well, not a new horse, but you know what I mean."

Stevie, still weighed down emotionally by Blake's departure, the looming sale of the ranch, and the thought that she would have to leave soon herself—Tulsa school classes started the next week; she wouldn't even know where "home" would be when she came back—had to ask Dad to repeat himself to make sure she had heard him right. Even then, she didn't see how it would work. "But what about school?"

Dad shrugged. "So you'll miss a day."

"More like three days," she said. "You'll have to come get me, and then take me back..." She let her voice fade away as she saw a smug smile forming on Dad's lips. "What?"

"If you want to go to school in Tulsa," Dad said, shrugging, "you can. I'll call Mary and let her know. But I already enrolled you here at Antlers—"

Stevie's squeal of delight and loving outrage cut him off, as did her hugging him tight across the chest. She paused her hug long enough to thump him in the chest—he deserved more, and harder, but she was too excited just then—and he laughed. The sound of his laughter making her even happier.

The next day, after Dr. Weaver gave her another checkup, and, shaking his head, said she was, "for lack of a better phrase, as healthy as a horse," Dad had helped her saddle up Rain for practice.

"I called Stan Harrison this morning," Dad said. "He said we could borrow Satchmo for the race. Satchmo's a damn—a great horse. Maybe even as fast as Jack Rabbit."

"Thanks," Stevie said, as she stepped into the stirrup and mounted Rain. "But I've already decided who I'll race." She patted Rain's neck. "You up to it, old girl?"

Rain snorted—then and now, as Stevie remembered—to show she was more than up to it. She would show the younger horses how barrel racing was done. *I was racing the barrels before you were born, little girl.*

"I know," Stevie said—then and now.

Dad—then and now—looked up at her curiously.

"Besides," Stevie had added at the time, "Jack Rabbit would never forgive me if I raced Satchmo."

Dad had just looked at her at that, as if she had spoken in some other language, then had shaken his head. But he hadn't argued.

It was like summer started all over again, even after the first day of school. Her and Dad working together on the ranch's few remaining chores or spending the day with Allison Keenan looking at other, smaller properties around Antlers. "A small place," Dad had told Allison. "Just big enough for me and Stevie—and Blake, when he's home. We need a barn, and a pasture big enough for the horses to run." Then in the late afternoons and evenings, they would saddle Rain and Buckaroo or Hobo or one of the other horses and ride. Just the two of them. Running the barrels, or just riding.

"You're up," Dad said, interrupting her thoughts. "Remember—"

"Barrel races are won in the turns. I got it."

Stevie and Rain moved into the starting chute.

Jack Rabbit had come home from Doc Siemers the week she started training again. Still sullen, keeping to himself, which was easier now that there were fewer than ten horses left on the ranch, almost never speaking to her. Still, when she went to see him yesterday afternoon before leaving for Muskogee, he had nuzzled her and blown gently in her face. As she hugged him, he replayed their first, winning race in her mind.

Win. The voice in her head, a young man's voice, was not one she had ever heard before. But she recognized Jack Rabbit immediately.

"I will," she had promised, hugging him.

We will, Rain said, bringing her back to the present.

The starting flag flashed through the air and they were off. Horse and girl surged forward.

As she had been taught by Blake—and Dad—they angled toward the first barrel, aiming at the point halfway between the first and third barrels.

She and Rain ran as one, horse and rider conjoined, charging at the barrels together, tightening for the turn toward the first barrel without even thinking about it. She saw the floor of the arena across Rain's neck, and she saw the barrels as if she were Rain. She gripped the reins in her hands and felt her feet in the stirrups, and she felt the sand of the arena crunch beneath Rain's hooves and felt her own weight on Rain's back, and she breathed in the warm air in two sets of lungs.

Maybe because she was so focused on the race, or maybe because she was so open to Rain, she found that she heard the other horses more clearly than ever before, and there were images in her mind that could not have come from Rain.

Stevie saw herself riding Rain, leaning forward in the saddle, one arm close to her body, the other extended, Rain's body stretched long and brown. And there was more than one set of images, each from a different angle, but all of them in sync. At the same time as she saw herself racing, she saw, overlaying both her and Rain, a younger Rain and older version of herself.

Stevie forced herself to keep her eyes on the barrel coming at her, to think only of the race in front of her. Yet still she saw herself and Rain take the first turn as if she watched from all sides of the arena. And she saw the younger Rain and the older Stevie take the same turn at the same time in the same way. Multiple exposures of *déjà vu* in full motion. Two Rains, teeth bared, neck curving into the turn, muscles tensed, hooves planted, and two Stevies, the same mixed expressions of concentration and exhilaration as she pushed against the stirrups and pulled against the reins.

They came out of the first turn and the sense of *déjà vu* continued. It was as if she was racing herself.

Only then did she realize the older version of herself wasn't Stevie Buckbee at all. It was Mom, the original Stephane Buckbee. A younger version of Mom, one still becoming the beauty she would be, one that Stevie had only seen in photographs.

She was racing Mom.

Stevie nearly lost her concentration, nearly caused Rain to misstep. But only nearly. Both horse and rider retained control. Stevie leaned even closer to Rain's neck and urged Rain to go faster, to try to get ahead of the vision. Rain responded. Stevie could feel the extra stretch and strain in her own muscles, but it was as if the memory of Mom had urged the younger Rain to the same additional effort. Both horses and both riders took the second turn at the same time in the same way, horses and riders as one.

Frustration mounted in Stevie as she and Rain remained in lock step with the vision in the rapid approach to the last barrel and the final turn. *I'm not like my mother!* she wanted to shout. She didn't know she had done it, but in the images in her mind she saw she was baring her teeth—and saw her mother wore the identical expression—as the four of them, past and present, took the third turn, all four of them wanting to win.

Coming around the last barrel, the shocks of memory and realization jolting her spine as much as the impact of Rain's hooves on the sand, Stevie caught a glimpse Dad and Blake standing at the front of the bleachers, cheering with their hands in the air. They looked happy. Happier than Stevie had seen them in years.

And suddenly, seeing them happy, Stevie was happy too.

She might look like Mom—some, she didn't think she was that pretty. She might ride like Mom. But she wasn't Mom.

She was Stevie.

She still wanted to win, though.

Stevie and Rain charged through the last leg of the race. In her mind, she saw Mom and the younger Rain running alongside, the differences between the two pairs clear now even as they crossed the finish line at almost the same time. Mom, the better, more experienced rider on the much younger horse, *might* have been a few inches ahead of her.

Stevie and Rain were both panting, Stevie still in the saddle holding the reins, when Dad and Blake came running up to her—and now she noticed that Shannon was there with Blake as well. Would the girl never learn she wasn't good enough for Blake?

Stevie pulled her right leg over and slid out of the saddle and into Dad's arms. "You did great, baby," Dad said, hugging her tight. "You did great!"

Stevie hugged him back. Then asked, "What was my time?"

No one had thought to look—or maybe Shannon said "17.05" and Stevie ignored her—but Stevie realized she didn't care so much about winning as Blake hugged her. Dad was there. Blake was there. Winning or not—having to hug Shannon or not—the only way it could've been more perfect was if Edwin had been there too. And maybe he was. She liked to think so.

Stevie accepted her second place trophy with—she thought—considerable grace.

The new Buckbee Ranch was smaller than half the south pasture of the original. But there was a house, a barn, a corral big enough to set up a practice barrel run, and a large enough pasture for Rain, Jack Rabbit and the other remaining horses to run. Travis helped Stevie and Dad move out of the old house and into the new one. Michelle was there when Stevie finally opened the birthday card from Mom and put it on a shelf in her new bedroom along with the other seven birthday cards and the summer's two trophies.

She and Dad had been in the new house for a week when Travis came around after school and found her sitting on the pasture fence, looking at the horses bunched in the center of the pasture.

"Are you going to run with the horses today?" Travis asked, leaning against the fence a few feet away, resting his forearms on the top bar. He looked up at her.

Instead of answering, she kicked out her left leg and flexed her ankle so he could more properly admire her new cross trainers. In spite of the September warmth, she wore loose-fitting jeans—in case she fell again, she didn't want to skin her knees—so he couldn't ogle her legs. Which was too bad. She still had a great tan, and the various scars from the summer had healed. Mostly. Her ankle looked cute, though, she thought.

Travis looked at the shoe—and at her exposed ankle, she was sure—and then back at her. "Does that mean 'yes'?"

"Yes," Stevie said. "I wasn't expecting an audience, though." Even if she had been hoping for one. She wouldn't tell him that. She was still getting used to admitting it to herself. She bit her lip. "I was never sure it wasn't a dream," she said. "The first time."

"Yeah," Travis said.

She looked at him, and into his big brown eyes. She wondered what went on in his mind. What did he really think of her? Would he ever try to kiss her again?

"I felt the same way," he added, keeping her gaze. A smile pulled at the corners of his lips. "Right up until you faceplanted in the dirt."

"Bah." Stevie looked away, her face getting warm. She glanced back just long enough to stick her tongue out at him, then pushed off the top of the fence and jumped down. The wooden fence shuddered as she pushed against it and her shoes raised little clouds of dust as she landed.

Rain and Jack Rabbit and Buckaroo and Hobo and the rest waited for her as she walked up, then clustered around her, nuzzling and blowing softly. Jack Rabbit was still recovering, but at least he had his cast off now. And he could run. Maybe in the spring she could ride him again. For now, though, she was happy to run with him.

"Try not to trip this time," Travis called to her.

In the middle of her herd, her family of horses, she didn't answer him. She stroked Jack Rabbit's nose. "Ready to run, boy?"

Jack Rabbit—all of them—whinnied and pranced. Then all of them, as one, started to run. The low thunder of the hooves grew and surrounded her as they raced. The September wind blew her hair back. Stevie still didn't know how she did this impossible thing, but she ran. With Jack Rabbit on her left and Rain on her right and all her horses around her.

She laughed as she ran. She felt the sunshine and the earth, smelled the sweat and the dust, with her own senses and those of the herd. She wondered if Mom had ever run with the horses this way. She wondered what Travis thought as he watched her. She wondered if she would ever tell Dad and Blake. But mostly she just laughed as she ran, thinking nothing, feeling everything. Running.

Travis was still there, leaning against the fence when the herd finally came to rest again. Stevie put an arm around Jack Rabbit's neck for support as she walked off the exertion, panting. She was smiling so much she thought her face might split as she looked at Travis. She wasn't sure she had ever been this happy. Even with this much dust in her mouth.

"I didn't," she said, still panting. She spat out some of the dust. "I didn't trip."

She saw the look on Travis's face, and she laughed.

THE END

Of

The Girl Who Ran With Horses

About the Author

David R. Michael likes to think he is amusing. He lives in Tulsa, Oklahoma, with his wife, kids, and cats, who more or less put up with him and sometimes humor him.

To know when new books by David R. Michael are available, sign up for his email newsletter here:

www.gunsandmagic.com

About the Cover

Cover painting, *Communion*, by Don Michael, Jr.

See more of Don's artwork here:

www.donmichaeljr.com

The Girls of Spring Hollow

People with fairy blood in their veins should be careful when saying, "I wish..."

Faye Woods and her little brother, Flub, are the newest residents of quirky, beautiful Spring Hollow, a neighborhood where the houses have names like Hawkbriar and Jack Rabbit Run--and where a hole in a park fence leads to Spring Hollow's magical Other Side.

Brenna Guin and Lupe Garcia have lived in Spring Hollow all their lives, but they have never seen anything like what they find when they follow Faye and Flub through the hole in the fence.

When an evil shadow from Spring Hollow's past emerges from the Other Side to threaten Flub, Faye and Brenna and Lupe must work together to rescue Flub before the sun rises.

Spring Hollow has always been haunted. Tonight the ghosts step out of the shadows!

The night before her annual July 4th Sleepover Extravaganza, Brenna Guin discovers her house is haunted by the ghost of a magician. Which, she decides, is perfect. A touch of ghostly magic is exactly the surprise her party needs—but something goes wrong.

First, one of her friends becomes a living ghost. Then every ghost in the Spring Hollow Cemetery comes to her party—and not just the friendly ones!

Now Brenna, with the help of her friends Lupe and Faye, must protect her sleepover guests from restless spirits while she races against the clock to rescue a ghost held prisoner—all before sunrise, when her parents wake up.

The Girls of Spring Hollow

Under the last Full Moon of summer, in the Overlap of Worlds, the Red Moon Faire opens its gates.

Lupe Garcia has never heard of the Red Moon Faire. All she knows is her dream of being a dog and chasing rabbits around Spring Hollow has turned out to be all too real.

She has no idea how to change back into her normal girl shape, and now the ghost of a saber-toothed tiger is chasing *her*.

Eluding the ghost, Lupe stumbles into the Overlap and the Faire. She's still a dog, but the Faire doesn't care. Everyone—and every*thing*—is welcome at the Red Moon Faire.

But there are also shadows at the Faire, and snares for the unwary. And a prisoner desperate to escape--even if the attempt puts Lupe in harm's way...

A new witch has come to Spring Hollow, just in time for Halloween.

Halloween is Brenna Guin's favorite time of year. With her new friends, Faye and Lupe, plus her new abilities--like being able to see in the dark--this year should be the best Halloween ever. If only her mother would stop ruining it for her.

Two nights before Halloween, sneaking out after dark--alone, because even Norv, her pet rat, refuses to cooperate--Brenna encounters Eve Coronelle, the neighborhood's newest addition.

Ever since Eve moved into the quaint gray brick house on Gingerbread Row, Brenna's mother has had nothing nice to say about the woman. Her mother had called Eve a witch more than once.

Turns out, her mother was right ...

www.ingramcontent.com/pod-product-compliance
Lightning Source LLC
Chambersburg PA
CBHW051250250626
47155CB00009B/3245